ROAD to TOMORROW

ROAD
to
TOMORROW

MARY METCALFE

Copyright © 2012 by Mary Metcalfe

First Edition – October 2012

ISBN (Paperback): 978-0-9879300-0-2
ISBN (eBook): 978-0-9879300-1-9

Published by:
Laskin Publishing
54 impasse Roy
St-Emile-de-Suffolk, QC
Canada J0V 1Y0

www.lakefrontmuse.ca

Distributed to the trade by The Ingram Book Company
Cover Design: Travis Miles, *ProBookCovers.com*
Interior Design and Layout: *www.wordzworth.com*

ACKNOWLEDGEMENTS

So many people have supported my writing habit the past couple of years. Thanks go to my whole extended family – Chenail, Nazarko, Fife, Barrett, Ford, Trépanier, Patterson and Wilson – plus my wonderful circle of friends.

Thanks to my editor Warren Layberry. You have made so many excellent suggestions that have improved my novels.

Special thanks for advice on traumatic brain injuries (TBI) to my new friends Sheri de Grom and Ron Dahl. Sheri also provided invaluable advice on military protocols regarding separation from service. Thanks too, to Jo-Anne Vienneau for her poignant memoir *Life Changes in a Fraction of a Second*, about her journey with her husband through their continuing life-changing adaptations resulting from her husband's severe TBI. I felt their pain and participated in their journey vicariously. Thanks also to Jon Katz for his wonderful books about Bedlam Farm and his special relationship with his working border collie Rose. My Rosie is for you, Jon.

To my great beta readers: Jude Driscoll, Glynis Smy, Sheri de Grom and Len Smith: Thank you so much for your excellent and thoughtful feedback. As Rosie knows, "That'll do."

Finally, as always, to my wonderful husband and very best friend Jacques Chenail, who is now a willing and eager proofreading partner. I'm glad you liked the story, dear. You're hired!

DEDICATION

This novel is lovingly dedicated to the memory of my aunt Helen "Tony" French, a successful screenwriter and former CBC Literary Competition judge, who suffered from life-changing TBI after being hit by an uninsured driver with a suspended license. The aftermath of her chronic brain injuries abruptly ended her writing and literary judging career.

PROLOGUE
SPRING 2006

ANDREA PUT ANOTHER BOX IN THE TRUNK OF HER '96 TOYOTA and went back for the suitcases. Emily and Simon were asleep in their car seats. She looked up from the sidewalk and saw Sean standing in the doorway, his tattooed muscular arms folded across his chest. Before she could say anything, he leaned over and picked up her two large suitcases and disappeared inside the brownstone.

Oh God! What's he doing now?

Running up the aging wooden steps, Andrea looked for him. "Sean? Where are you?"

She heard water running and ran up the dingy carpeted stairs to the second floor. *What the hell is he doing?*

The bathroom door was closed. She turned the handle and pushed with all her might, but it wouldn't budge. *He's leaning against it.* She could hear the bathwater running and pounded her fist on the door. "Sean, open the door. Please."

An acrid smell reached her nostrils and made her eyes tear up. She pounded on the door again. *God, please. I can't stay here another day. I have to get away. He's going to kill me.*

She pounded with both hands on the door as steam began to emerge around the frame. After a minute, she stopped and leaned against the wall. She slumped to the floor, her head in her hands.

"Why are you doing this to me? Why can't you just let me leave?" *He'll make it look like an accident. An accidental overdose. A suicide. He keeps telling people I have postpartum depression.*

Minutes later, the bathroom door was quietly opened. Clouds of steam billowed out. Andrea raised her head and watched Sean walk away without a word. As she stood up, she heard him open the fridge door and pop open a can of beer. *If I'm lucky, he'll just fall asleep in his chair.*

She already knew what she'd find. She walked into the still-steamy room, and there, in the bathtub, were all her best clothes—stewing in a pool of water the color of an angry bruise. Her cotton shirts, wool sweaters and pants, and silk blouses were ruined, their colors bleeding as the bleach-laden water sucked the life out of them.

He's beaten me again, without even touching me. Andrea's face showed no emotion as she went back down the stairs. She saw Sean sitting in his chair with his beer, watching baseball. The children were still in the car. She could hear them crying and went to them, tears streaming down her cheeks.

CHAPTER ONE

IT WAS A LOVELY SPRING MORNING as Andrea buckled Emily and Simon into their car seats. "What a gorgeous day. Listen to all the birds, Emily."

"I want to see Uncle Richard's cat. She purrs really loud." Emily hugged her teddy bear. "Mommy, can I have a snack at Uncle Richard's?"

"You sure can. Maybe they'll have some cookies." Andrea willed herself to keep her voice light as she drove the short distance to her brother's home. "You haven't been on a sleepover at Uncle Richard's for a long time. Are you excited?"

"Yes! I like it when he lets me sit on his shoulders, way up high." Emily reached up both arms and waved them around in the small car.

"Oh, look. He's waiting for us." Andrea pulled the car up to the curb in front of a tidy brick townhouse. Her twin was already down the steps and opening the back door as Andrea got out. He unbuckled Emily and helped her out of her car seat.

"How's my dancing Peanut?"

"I'm fine, Uncle Richard. But I think my teddy bear has a cold and needs a cookie." Emily held out the bear for examination.

"Hmm, I think you're right. Aunt Louise knew you were coming. She made a batch of peanut butter cookies." Richard reached into the back seat and retrieved a couple of bags. "She's at work right now, but she'll be home for supper."

"Emily, go ahead with your Uncle. I'll bring Simon in." She turned back to her sleeping toddler and released his car seat.

ANDREA LOOKED UP into her brother's eyes. She was cupping a steaming mug of coffee in her hands. "Thanks so much for agreeing to take care of Emily and Simon until I get settled somewhere."

3

"I wish you'd reconsider this, Andy," he said, using her pet name. "At least try marriage counseling. You don't know what he's seen over there or what he's had to do. He has to have PTSD. I've had some issues, myself." Richard looked into soft hazel eyes that matched his own.

"But you don't slap Louise around or drink yourself blind almost every night."

"No, I don't." Richard took in a deep breath and sighed. "I'm just saying, give him a chance to be the kind of guy he used to be."

"The one who slapped me around on our honeymoon?" Andrea shook her head. "We had problems from the start. It's gotten worse. He refuses to admit he has serious issues." Andrea watched Emily feeding her bear some cookie. Simon was still sound asleep in his car seat on the couch beside her.

"You know what happened when I tried to leave him before. I can't be here when he gets back."

"Where are you going?"

"I'd rather not tell you. That way, you won't have to lie. I'll be in touch with my new email address. I don't want Sean harassing me by email."

Looking over at her son, who would always remind her of his father, Andrea tried to quell her pounding pulse. *I can't believe it. I'm going to get away this time.*

"What do I tell Sean?" Richard glanced around at the sound of a loud meow. "Look Emily. Sushi's coming to see you."

"Tell him I can't live with the emotional and physical abuse." Andrea felt tears threatening to well up and pushed them back. "Tell him I'm lodging a complaint with Family Advocacy."

"You know it could affect his career?"

"I know, but my life and the safety of the children come first."

"Then why not take them with you, now?"

"I need to figure out my life, Richard. I lost myself the past few years. I used to be a confident person with career ambitions. I love my children but not at the expense of what I've become." Andrea stared into her murky brown coffee. "I want to be the best mother I can be, but right now, I can't. This past month, as it got closer and closer to him coming back, I came undone. I can't sleep. I'm breaking things. My nerves are shot. I can't take any more."

"Maybe you're the one that needs help. Maybe you've just burned out with handling the kids alone. Maybe Family Advocacy could help you with that." Emily was absorbed with the loudly purring cat on her lap.

Andrea spoke under her breath. "Richard, listen. It's not about the kids. It's not about me. It's about Sean. He's an abuser. And I'm not taking it even one more day."

"Okay, okay, I get your point. I just hoped that you two would make a good life together. You're my only sister, and he's my best buddy." Richard reached across the table and put his hand over hers. "But, I've got your back. I'll help you deal with Sean."

Andrea reluctantly left Emily and Simon. Richard held Emily's hand as they stood on the porch to wave goodbye. Andrea let out her breath slowly and went back to her car. "You do everything Uncle Richard tells you, okay sweetie?"

"I will, Mommy."

"And give my love and thanks to Louise." She got into the car and took one last look at her three-year-old, then pulled away, tears clouding her vision. *Goodbye, my babies.* She held her free hand over her heart and drew a ragged breath. *I'll be back for you as soon as I can.*

IT WAS ALMOST AN HOUR before she could stop her hands from trembling and another half hour before her sobbing cries slowed and finally stopped. *I've abandoned my children. What will people think of me?* She dabbed at her eyes. *I can't expect anyone to forgive me, especially Emily and Simon. But I just don't see any other way.*

She stopped for gas and then continued driving northeast, passing trees covered in pastel green buds. Crossing from Connecticut into Massachusetts, she realized there was no turning back. She stopped in Springfield and bought a sandwich and coffee.

She pressed the cold, wrapped sandwich against a puffy eye, feeling numb with grief. *I have to stay strong. My children deserve better than this. I deserve better than this.* She slowly unwrapped the sandwich, took one bite, and set it aside.

Back on the highway, the stress of the past few weeks gradually took its toll. Andrea drove on, oblivious to the soft, natural beauty around her. As the afternoon slipped towards evening, she pressed on, determined to reach her destination.

Carol Brock and her business partner Flynn were driving home from a long day at their gift shop.

"Are you sure you and Gregory wouldn't like to stay for dinner? Devin said he's doing Thai tonight." Carol guided her car along the winding country road towards home. "He always does enough for at least six and we've both had a long day."

"Thanks for the offer, sweetie, but I've planned a special dinner just for two. It's the anniversary of the day we first met."

"How long have you two been together now?"

"Twenty years today," Flynn said. "We've been married fifteen."

"You two were real groundbreakers back in those days, weren't you?"

"Indeed we were. Still are for some people." Flynn patted Carol's arm. "I was thrilled when Devin brought you home. But, I never dreamed I'd be in business with his Boston beauty. It's working out so well sometimes I have to pinch myself to remind me this is real."

Carol chuckled. "Well you can stop. It's real. And, I can tell you working at the store beats just about anything from my former career. It's a lot of work but it's fun."

They were chatting about their next buying trip, when they saw the dim taillights of a vehicle in the ditch.

"Oh God," Carol said, "Call 911 and put out some flares. They're in the trunk." She brought her BMW to a skidding halt, then jumped out and ran back towards the upended car, leaving Flynn to search for the flares. Carol gasped as she went up to her knees in frigid ditch water from the spring melt.

Reaching the driver's side, she pounded on the window and was rewarded with slow movement of the driver's head. She pulled the door open, as water poured in around the driver's feet and ankles. Carol put her hand in to brace the woman's head.

Flynn set up several flares and ran back to the car.

"She's barely conscious," Carol spoke over her shoulder. "Go on ahead to the house. Ask Devin to come. And ask him to bring me some dry shoes and socks. I'll stay with her and wait for the paramedics."

She turned back to the woman in the car who was now moaning and trying to move. "Stay still. You've been in a car accident. You need to stay very still."

Carol watched in alarm as the young woman's eyes slowly opened and twitched uncontrollably. "Please, be still. You have a head injury. My name is Carol. What's your name?"

Her voice came out in a faint whisper. "Andrea. My name is Andrea." A distant siren could now be heard.

"Andrea, you're going to be fine. An ambulance is coming." Carol smoothed her hand over the woman's thick wavy hair. She was shivering from the cold and her feet were going numb. "Where are you from?"

Andrea moaned. Carol kept stroking her head, moving dark curls away from her forehead, where a nasty gash was oozing blood. Looking up, she could see flashing lights coming down the dark road.

Overhead, a canopy of twinkling stars and a small sliver of moonlight gave faint illumination. Her legs were now going numb. *At least it isn't raining,* she thought, as dark clouds scudded across the twinkling sky.

Moments later, she stepped back as the volunteer firefighters took over. She was climbing out of the muddy ditch when she noticed bright headlights bumping down the lane across the road. A moment later, her husband pulled up in his pickup.

"Is the driver okay?" Devin walked over to hug his shivering wife. "I brought you dry socks and loafers."

A burly firefighter walked over to them. "Evenin' Devin, Evenin' Ms. Brock. I think she'll be okay. My guess is she fell asleep at the wheel and drifted off the road slowly. No signs of braking. Road conditions are normal. If she's lucky, it's just a nasty concussion from hitting her head on the steering wheel. The car's too old for airbags."

A loud siren announced the approaching ambulance. A paramedic soon joined them as her partner put a brace around Andrea's neck. "Do you folks know her?"

"No," Carol said, "none of us do. Her first name is Andrea."

"Her ID says she's Andrea Garrett from Newark." The paramedic held the woman's wallet in her hand.

More flashing lights heralded the arrival of a state trooper. The squad car pulled in behind the downed car. A young female officer emerged and strode over, her powerful flashlight illuminating the scene. "Everything under control here?"

"I figure she fell asleep at the wheel. No sign of alcohol." The firefighter and police officer shook hands.

"I'll run her plates." The officer took the wallet and license and walked back to her cruiser. Moments later she returned. "She's Andrea Sharon Garrett." She wrote her details down as the firefighters gently transferred the small unconscious figure out of her car and into the arms of the paramedics, who laid her on a stretcher at the side of the road. "I'll call for towing. Where to?"

"No need. I have a tractor. We'll pull it out and check it over in daylight and see what the damage is." Devin walked over to look at the front end of the car.

"Where are you taking her?" Carol asked the paramedic and then looked at Devin as he came back to stand beside her. He nodded at her unspoken question.

"St. Luke's is the closest."

"We'll follow you. She shouldn't be alone." Carol sat on the bumper of the pickup to change into the dry socks and shoes.

"Appreciate it." The paramedic headed back to the ambulance. The ambulance was soon speeding along the country road towards the hospital. Devin and Carol quickly lost track of the flashing lights as they followed in the pickup.

"SHE'S LUCKY. NOTHING IS BROKEN, but she's going to have headaches for a few days and will need to be closely monitored for the next twenty-four hours." The emergency room resident looked questioningly at Carol and Devin. "We'll keep her here for observation, but I wonder if I could speak to you in the hall." He motioned them both away from the bed where Andrea lay dozing, pale and small in the bed.

"I realize you don't know her, but we've left a message at her home. It's her voice on the service. We have no way of knowing if she lives alone until she fully regains consciousness. She's not wearing a wedding ring." The resident looked at both of them. "She's from out-of-state and doesn't have any evidence of medical coverage. I probably can't keep her here more than overnight. My hands are pretty tied."

"We'll bring her back to our farm. She can stay with us until we get her story." Carol said. "We'll take responsibility for her bill."

Devin and Carol linked hands and smiled at each other. "We have a daughter about her age."

The resident nodded. "Someone will call you when she can be released. Probably mid-afternoon tomorrow if there are no complications. The resident on duty will sign the discharge papers and give you a phone number. If you have any concerns about her condition, page it, day or night. She should be checked on every two hours for another day."

"Thank you, doctor," Carol looked at Devin. "Guess we'd better get home. I don't know about you, but I'm starving. It's been hours since I ate."

"Me too. Let's get home and salvage what's left of the evening." Devin draped his arm over her shoulder.

ANDREA OPENED HER EYES AND LOOKED AT THE MONITOR BESIDE THE BED. Then she gazed around the room. There were several curtained cubicles. She could hear monitors beeping. Somewhere, someone was wheezing, almost gasping for breath. Nurses with trolleys flitted past on silent soles. She could just see part of a window from her bed. It was daylight. She had a vague memory of being in an accident and being lifted into an ambulance. A nurse came in.

"Where am I?" Andrea looked up at the nurse.

"You're at St. Luke's hospital in New Bedford, Massachusetts, Andrea. Do you remember the car accident?"

"Sort of. Well, not really." Andrea watched as the nurse checked her IV lines. "Where's my purse?"

The nurse was handing the shoulder bag to Andrea when Carol walked in.

"Hello, Andrea, that's quite the shiner." Carol smiled as she walked into the curtained off area around the bed. "Do you remember me? I'm Carol Brock. I found your car in the ditch last evening."

Andrea focused her eyes on Carol with some effort and gave her a tentative smile. "I don't remember your face, but I recognize your voice. Thank you for helping me."

"We're not finished. You're coming home with us. The hospital called your home and left a message, but there's been no response."

Andrea's eyes suddenly grew round. Her breathing became rapid just as the monitor beeped an alarm. Carol watched as Andrea began shaking uncontrollably. She quickly stood back as the nurse moved forward.

"What happened? She was fine a minute ago." The nurse muted the beeping machine as the resident rushed over and checked the readings.

"She's hyperventilating." He turned to look at Andrea and spoke firmly. "Andrea. Listen to me. Take deep breaths."

"She seems to be having a panic attack." The resident looked at Carol.

"I told her the hospital was trying to reach her home." She frowned and looked at Andrea, who was now hiccupping as she tried to control her breathing.

"Andrea. Keep taking slow, deep breaths." The doctor put his hand on her arm. She put her hand over her mouth as the hiccups continued. She looked up at them, her eyes wide with fear.

"My husband is coming back from Afghanistan." She swallowed nervously. "I left him. I don't want him to know where to find me."

The resident straightened up. He glanced at Carol then reached up and rubbed the back of his neck for a few seconds while he thought. "I can put you in touch with the hospital's social worker."

"Andrea, I'm so sorry." Carol walked around to the other side of the bed and sat down on a chair. She reached out and took Andrea's hand in hers. It felt small and cold. "Come and stay on my farm until you're better. My best friend used to be a social worker in Boston. We'll help you."

Carol looked up at the resident. "I suggest you put a notice on her file to refer any calls about her to the police. That will slow him down when he finds out about the accident and give us time to get a plan together."

The resident looked relieved. "I can do that."

Carol looked at Andrea, who wasn't much older than Ashley. "Andrea, look at me."

Andrea winced in pain as she turned to look at Carol. "I don't want him to be able to find me. I think he might kill me."

"You're a brave young woman. It took a lot of courage to do what you did. We're going to help you get your life back. Do you believe me?"

Andrea took a cautious breath. "Yes, I believe you."

As Devin helped Andrea into his pickup at the hospital entrance, Carol called Flynn. "We're bringing Andrea Garrett home with us. We should be there in about half an hour." She looked at the young woman's slumped shoulders as they all buckled up and Devin pulled away. "And if you wouldn't mind putting out something for us to eat, that would be great."

Andrea watched Carol tuck her iPhone back into her purse. "When I left New Jersey yesterday afternoon, I just wanted to get to Boston and get lost in the city. I can't believe how everything changed so fast."

Carol smiled. "Devin here was sent into my life at the right time just over a year ago. Sometimes, the universe helps you meet the people you need in your life."

"Thank you for caring about a stranger." Andrea said, leaning into Carol. As they drove back to the farm, a light rain started to fall.

"Stick with us, and you'll find there are a lot of people around here who care about strangers." Devin patted her knee. "And you're about to meet one of the best of them."

When they pulled up to a large Victorian farmhouse, half an hour later, Flynn glided down the verandah stairs to meet them.

"Is this the little duckling who landed in the ditch? Oooh, what a nasty shiner." Flynn peered at Andrea, who managed a weak smile. "Let's get a fresh ice pack on that. Yours has melted."

"What a beautiful home," Andrea looked around in awe as Flynn helped her into a large, brightly-lit kitchen brimming with enticing aromas. She stared at the gleaming granite counters and stainless steel appliances. "It's huge compared to what we live in."

Carol came up behind her and smiled. "It's big but cozy, don't you think?"

"It *is* cozy."

Andrea went straight to the nearest chair and sat down, dropping her shoulder bag on the floor beside her as Flynn pulled a gel pack from the freezer and handed it to her.

"I hope you have an appetite, sweetie. I'm reheating an eggplant parmesan. Didn't know when Devin and Carol would be back."

Andrea blinked and shook her head slightly. She immediately winced. "It smells heavenly, but I'm not really hungry."

Flynn fussed around his patient as Carol said, "The doctor suggested that you eat a little bit at a time and see how it goes." Andrea looked at the large pine table that was already set for three. *They've given up two evenings in a row to take care of me.*

"Why are you doing this for me?" she asked. "You don't even know me."

"My daughter Ashley is probably just a couple of years younger than you. I'm just a momma bear protecting a wounded cub. Your husband will have to go through me before he can get anywhere near you."

"There's something I need to tell you." Andrea lowered her eyes and hung her head.

Carol and Flynn exchanged a look.

"What is it, Andrea?" Devin asked, gently.

"I left my husband, but I also left my two children." Unshed tears stung Andrea's eyes. She felt a lump forming in her throat. *I need to be with my babies. They must be wondering why I'm not with them.*

"I have a daughter, Emily. She's almost four. Simon is eighteen months old." She looked up at the three of them as tears spilled over her pale cheeks.

"Oh, Andrea." Carol walked over and put an arm around her shoulder.

"I knew if I took them with me that he would hunt us to the ends of the earth." Andrea cried quietly with her head in her hands. "He left me no choice. I had to leave the children and hope he won't come after me."

"Would you like some sparkling water?" Devin poured glasses of wine for himself and Carol. "You've tried to leave him before?"

"Thank you." Andrea accepted a glass of water and took a sip. "I've tried three times. Last time, I ended up in emergency with cracked ribs.

"We're just property to him. He owns us. We're his proof to the army that he is the kind of soldier they want. With a wife and two children, he's a poster-perfect military family man." Andrea looked at the plate of food that Flynn had put in front of her. "He wouldn't harm the children, but he will harm me. I think he would kill me if I tried to take the children."

Flynn shook his head and looked at them. "If it's okay with you, Andrea, I'll stay and check on you during the night. I think our store will be closed tomorrow for a family emergency. Will that work for you, Carol?"

"We'll take turns."

"You be the momma bear, Devin's the papa bear and I am uncle bear. The three bears will tuck you into bed and watch over you." Flynn patted Andrea's shoulder. "You're safe here."

"I know." Andrea sighed and blew her nose. Tasting some of the eggplant parmesan, she discovered that she was hungry after all. "This sure beats the hospital food."

"Speaking of the hospital, could you call in and delete the message?"

Andrea looked at the clock. "He's home by now and has probably already picked up the message because I wasn't there to pick him up with the kids.

"I'll give it a try though." Andrea took the portable Carol handed her and dialed a central number. After entering her code, she listened briefly and shook her head. "It's saying no new messages."

"He knows you're in this area." Carol sipped her wine. "I think having him referred to the police should head him off."

Andrea looked at the three of them and sighed. "Don't count on it."

CHAPTER TWO

"HOW'S THE HEAD TODAY?" Carol was drinking her second morning coffee when Andrea padded into the kitchen in borrowed slippers and a dressing gown.

"Nothing half a bottle of aspirin won't take care of." Andrea smiled, thinly. "It was quite a shock seeing myself in a mirror, let me tell you."

"Let's get you a cup of coffee and go sit in the solarium. I think you'll enjoy the view." Carol poured. "How do you take it?"

"A splash of milk, please." Andrea gazed around again at the large, bright kitchen. "This looks like it came out of a magazine. It's so beautiful."

"Flynn and Devin designed it before I met them. I had the same reaction as you. I used to be a real estate agent in Boston, so I know my kitchens. Follow me." Carol picked up her mug and Andrea's and led the way into a spacious solarium. "Come and see the horses."

Andrea crossed the room and saw a paddock not fifty feet away, where two tall horses and a somewhat shorter one were grazing. "They're magnificent. Is this a ranch?"

"No, it's a hobby farm. We're on fifty acres." Carol pointed to the tallest horse, "The one with the cream-colored tail is Aerosmith. We call him Aero. The one next to him is Sabrina and the short one is Pablo. Do you ride?"

"I did some trail riding when I was a kid. Whenever we went on vacation, I wanted to find a place to go riding. I was maybe ten years old the first time." Andrea watched the horses with fascination. "My father was a veterinarian. I'm a veterinary technician who's never worked in my field."

"What happened?"

Andrea sighed and gazed out the window. "My parents were killed in a car accident when I was in third year. Somehow, I managed to graduate." She sipped at her coffee. "After, I went to New Jersey and lived with my twin brother Richard and his new wife. They introduced me to Sean and then all my plans changed. I became an army wife who got pregnant within weeks of being married."

"Sean is your husband?"

"Yes," she said.

"What are your plans now?"

"Hire a good lawyer. I want a divorce and I want my children with me and nowhere near him." Andrea spoke with conviction. "Sean is an abusive bully. He doesn't deserve to have the children with him. I don't want Simon to turn out like his father, that's for sure."

The early spring sunshine was doing its best to warm the solarium as the two women talked, enjoyed their coffee and watched the horses grazing in misty solitude.

"How about we get you some breakfast?" Carol led them back to the kitchen and went to the refrigerator. "When did you first realize he was an abuser?"

"On our honeymoon. He got drunk and backhanded me across the face when he thought I'd been too friendly with a lifeguard." Andrea slid half a bagel in the toaster and spooned colorful slices of strawberry and kiwi into a bowl. "I spent most of the week in our room because of the black eye and bruising. He didn't even remember doing it.

"He insisted on being with me when I was shopping for clothes. At first, I thought it was romantic. Then I realized he had to control everything. He chose what I would wear to base parties. Had to know where I was all the time. By that time, I was pregnant with Emily and we'd been transferred to another base." Andrea bit into a juicy red strawberry. "This is delicious, by the way."

Carol topped up her coffee and let Andrea talk.

"We moved so often I had no support network. My brother was posted overseas. Email contact was sporadic. I had to start all over, making new friends and getting our house in order each time we moved."

"You must've felt very isolated." Carol shook her head. "I can't imagine what you went through."

"At first, the physical abuse only happened when he was drinking. But after his second tour, when Simon was an infant, even small things would set him off. He made sure not to leave marks where they'd show. I was terrified for the children."

"Was there no one you could talk to?" Carol finished her breakfast but made no move to clear things away.

Andrea shook her head. "There's a Family Advocacy program but I kept hoping he would turn around. I was warned by other wives that, if I went public, it would end his military career. And, of course, he always apologized and promised not to do it again. I believed him for a while because I really wanted our marriage to work. Then, I stayed with him for the children."

"What made you leave this time?"

"Last time he was home, he told me it doesn't bother him to kill, including innocent civilians who get in his line of fire. He calls it collateral damage. What terrified me most was the look in his eyes. It was almost *feral*."

"Good God."

"Sean likes to kill people. I can't live with someone who doesn't value life. I can't bring up my children in that environment."

Carol nodded. "I couldn't live with someone like that either. Devin and I had an experience with someone who was ready to kill. It changed our lives, luckily for the better in our case. Let's hope it does for you, too.

"Listen, I have an idea about what you could do with that veterinary technology degree. We have a vet in the area who's always complaining that she doesn't have enough hours in her day. Maybe you could assist her."

"I worked with my father on weekends and summer holidays all through high school. I have a lot of experience around animals." Andrea gingerly brought some dishes to the sink.

"Here, I'll take care of things today." Carol took the dishes out of Andrea's hands. "Why don't you curl up with a book or a movie and just rest easy? I think my daughter's clothes will fit you if we roll up the pant legs. She's almost six feet tall."

Andrea chuckled and cradled her head with one hand. "I'm five-five. That'll take some rolling."

"For now, you don't even need to get dressed. Devin has gone into Boston for the day. Gregory never comes in the house and Flynn is one of the girls."

"Gregory is Flynn's partner?"

"Yes."

"Never see that on a base." Andrea smiled. "Flynn is such a good person. He was fussing over me like a mother hen during the night."

"That's Flynn." Carol deposited Andrea on the larger couch in the solarium and brought over some pillows and an afghan throw. "Book or movie?"

"Movie, please. Something that's not animated."

Carol laughed. "Bet you need a little mommy vacation."

"I really do." Andrea sighed and leaned back as Carol put a pillow behind her back. "I haven't been mothered in a long time. I'd forgotten what it feels like."

"Where are Sean's parents?"

"In British Columbia. I haven't seen them since Simon was a few months old. His mother and I never hit it off." Andrea shrugged. "She thought I was uppity for going to university and dreaming of a career. Now I know where Sean learned his poor attitude towards women."

"Do you know if his mother was abused?"

Andrea laughed ruefully and looked out at the grazing horses. "If anything, I'd say it's my father-in-law who's abused, emotionally at least. Lorna Garrett thinks the entire world revolves around her and her only child. In her eyes, he can do no wrong. What Sean wants, Sean gets."

"Oh boy. Sounds like a recipe for a spoiled brat."

"Who is also handsome, intelligent, charming when it suits him and won't let anyone or anything stand in the way of getting what he wants." Andrea watched as Aero and Sabrina rubbed their heads against each other. "And five years ago, what he wanted was me."

"Can't blame him. Under that shiner and bruising lies a very pretty face. Your driver's license photo is very flattering." Carol smiled warmly as she handed Andrea the remotes. "Listen, I need to do some errands. I'll be back in time to fix us some lunch. Flynn is coming by shortly. He'll be checking in on you."

"Thank you so much, Carol. And by the way, I have the money to pay you back for my hospital bill. At some point, I'll get my Tricare card and put in a claim."

"Don't worry about it. We'll settle up another day. You just rest easy and relax."

Andrea smiled as Carol met up with Flynn outside and gave him a hug before going to her car.

"IT LOOKS LIKE YOUR CAR IS A WRITE-OFF, SWEETIE." Flynn went over and sat beside Andrea in the sun-drenched room. He peered at her bruised face. "Your colors are coming in nicely though. Deep magenta, sea foam green and some dashes of indigo. I don't think we'll see the pastels for a couple of days yet."

Andrea smiled, even though her eyelids were heavy from the constant dull ache in her head. "Never thought of it that way, Flynn. You make it sound pretty."

"What will be pretty is you, when the bruising fades and we get you some new clothes. You didn't bring anything with you?"

"I wanted a complete new start. I inherited some money. I'm going to set myself up and start a new life with my children, as far away from an army base as I can get." Andrea smelled the aroma of something freshly-baked. "You baked after barely sleeping all night?"

"I made a batch of blueberry muffins. Brought some up for you to taste test." Flynn straightened some magazines. "Gregory and I have a small house near the east property line. I have a pretty decent kitchen, although this one is my dream."

"Carol said you helped design it, so it must be your dream kitchen." Andrea's face had the beginnings of a girlish grin. "I could probably eat a muffin. I can't resist that heavenly smell."

"With a glass of milk?"

"Sounds perfect." Andrea closed her eyes as Flynn walked

back to the kitchen. She heard him humming as he put together her snack. *I can't believe I'm eating again already!"*

"You say my car is finished?" Andrea smiled as she accepted the frothy milk and warm muffin. Flynn went to sit on a deep cushioned wicker armchair across from her.

"Gregory and Devin pulled it out with the tractor. We checked it over. The front axle on the passenger side is broken. There's a fair bit of body damage too. That ditch is deep."

"Mmm. This muffin is so delicious. I'm not much of a baker. Main meals are my forte, but simple ones. Nothing gourmet." Andrea smiled. "If you give me the number of the local towing service, I'll arrange to send it to a scrap yard."

"Already taken care of, sweetie. The tow truck should be here by noon." Flynn said. He stood and walked to the windows. "Even if it could be fixed, there's only one mechanic in this area and he's in demand."

"Funny, I still don't know where I am."

"We're about an hour and a half drive from Boston, near a little town named Laskin. You were heading for Boston weren't you?"

Andrea put her empty glass and plate on the nearby table. "I figured it would be a good place to raise my children. I never really liked Newark, but it's where my brother moved when he was called up. I was raised in the country. A place like this is much more what I like."

"Well, there's good child care and schools in the area. You couldn't go wrong living around here, and you'd be close to Boston for shopping." Flynn waved from the window to Gregory as he came out of the stable.

"Carol and I have a bookstore and gift shop in town. I heard there's an apartment for rent next to the Sweet Repose Bakery and Tea Room, just down the street from us. Can you imagine living next door to a bakery? They bake pies every day starting at six, then tarts and muffins. They also have fresh bread, rolls and croissants."

"Wouldn't need an alarm clock, that's for sure." Andrea smiled weakly and massaged the back of her neck. "Time for some more aspirin."

"I'll get it. Stay put, sweetie. You aren't going anywhere today."
Flynn returned with a tray holding a jug of ice water, a glass and the
bottle of aspirin. "Here you go, dear." He filled a glass, took two
pills out of the bottle and handed them to her.

"Thank you, nurse Flynn." Andrea said and washed down the
pills with the last of her milk. "I think I need to lie down for a while
until the pills take effect. Don't feel so good at the moment. My
stomach is fine though."

"Here, let's get these pillows rearranged." Flynn took the glass
away and then helped Andrea stretch out on the couch, with the
pillows under her head. "I'll call and find out about the apartment if
you're interested."

"I need at least a two-bedroom. Three would be perfect." Andrea spoke with her eyes closed. "If it came even partly furnished,
that would be a big help."

"I'm on it, sweetie. What's your budget?"

"For now, if it's the right apartment for me, I'll pay and deal
with my finances another day."

"Okay, I hear you." Flynn pulled down a couple of blinds to
shade the room. "Rest easy, Andrea."

"Thank you for everything, Flynn."

ANDREA WAS JARRED AWAKE by the sound of a tow truck lumber-
ing up the lane. Sitting up slowly, she held her hand against the side
of her head and took a moment to stand up. She walked over to the
window and raised one of the blinds. Outside, her wounded car
was being prepared for hoisting onto the bed of the truck. Within
minutes it had been secured on the flatbed.

"Hello, sleeping beauty." Carol walked in to the sunny room
and handed Andrea a slim laptop. "We took everything out of the
car. I have to say that front end doesn't look good at all. How old is
the car?"

"I've had it since university, and it was used when I got it. It's
going on fourteen years, I guess." Andrea looked on in dismay.
The front right wheel was turned at an impossible angle. "I've
been thinking about getting a van. The car's really not big enough

with the two kids and all their gear. Guess I don't have a choice now."

Carol put an arm around Andrea's thin muscled shoulder. "There's a little used car dealership outside Laskin. We'll go over when you're up to it if you like."

Andrea smiled and nodded her thanks. *This is going to eat into my cash reserves. I was hoping the car would make it another year or so.* She watched in silence as her only piece of physical freedom was taken away.

"FEEL UP TO GOING FOR A LITTLE WALK BEFORE SUPPER and meet the horses?" Carol could see Andrea's color was better and that she was walking on steadier feet after three days of house rest. "I'm sure we have a pair of shoes or boots that would fit you."

"My head still feels foggy. Some fresh air would be good. I'm not used to staying inside three days in a row. I'm always out with the kids at the park or playground."

"I'll just finish putting together the salad and we'll go find you some clothes. Devin said he'd be home by six. He's gone to sign a contract to restore an old homestead near here."

When the salad was finished, Carol rinsed her hands. "Ashley left a bunch of sweats and hoodies here. You can pick the color you want."

"Thanks, Carol. I can't wait to get into my 'to do' list. Flynn is positive the apartment is just what I'm looking for. Your friend Val called earlier and wants to see me as soon as I'm up to it." Andrea sat at the table. "I need to get a Massachusetts driver's license and buy a van. And I need to open a bank account, get money transferred to pay for everything and apply for my own credit card."

"You need a wife and secretary is what you need." Carol laughed as Andrea counted everything off on her fingers. "At least you have a laptop."

"I bought it when I decided I was going to leave Sean. I wanted everything I took with me to belong to me and not be something he gave me or bought us."

"I felt the same way when I kicked my first husband to the curb. I learned he was a serial cheater with women half his age. The last one was the final straw. She was only a few years older than Ashley. It disgusted me, so I kicked him out. Cost me a bundle."

"What do you mean it cost *you* a bundle?" Andrea looked confused. "He was the one cheating. Didn't he have to pay support?"

Carol grinned. "He had to pay support, yes. Lots of it. But I wouldn't take anything from our marriage, either. We sold the house and contents. I bought a three-bedroom condo and furnished it from top to bottom with the best designer furniture. That's what cost the bundle. But, by the time I was finished, there wasn't a single thing to remind me of him, except our kids."

"You know how I feel then."

"I know exactly how you feel. Right down to the last chair. The Goodwill people knew me by name by the time I was finished."

"Did it help?" Andrea steepled her fingers under her chin. "I mean, did it give you some closure?"

"Andrea, you won't know the true meaning of retail therapy until we get you out shopping in the next few days. You'll be a new woman by the time you're finished."

"That's what I'm counting on, Carol. A new woman is exactly what I want to be."

ANDREA APPROACHED THE HORSES QUIETLY, talking to them as she moved closer. "Look at you beauties. Aero, Sabrina, and Pablo. Such lovely names."

The horses looked at her with their ears pricked forward. Aero pawed the ground. "Someone takes very good care of you." Andrea came within a few feet of Aero, who had the lead position. Andrea watched him. When she sensed a slight agitation, she squatted down and kept speaking quietly.

"Hi there, Aero. I'm the new girl in town. It must be a bit confusing. I'm wearing Ashley's clothing, so I smell like Ashley but *I'm* not Ashley." She put her hand out with a carrot. "Maybe this will help convince you I'm a friend though."

She stayed quiet without moving. It was Pablo who ambled over and scored the carrot first. "Hello, Pablo. I hear some people call you a pony. But you really are a very fine horse." She stood up slowly and reached up to stroke the small horse's luxuriant blonde mane. She ignored Aero.

A moment later, she felt warm breath behind her. Turning slowly, she looked up into Aero's nostrils and then into his liquid brown eyes. "Aero's a little jealous. Either that, or he wants a carrot, too."

Gregory and Carol watched as all three horses hovered over the petite woman. Gregory spoke first.

"I've been with these horses since Devin brought them home. I've never seen them be this trusting so fast. Aero normally holds back. He's Devin's horse through and through."

Carol ran her hands through her hair and smiled in wonder. "Her father was a veterinarian. She worked weekends and summers with him."

"That wouldn't explain this. She's a horse whisperer. Second one I've seen." Gregory watched as the three horses followed meekly behind Andrea as if they were dogs. "Kyle Sheridan is the other. Aero likes to think he's in charge, even with Devin."

"Well, it's pretty clear who's in charge right now. All five and a half feet of her," Carol chuckled.

"I'M GOING TO FILE A MISSING PERSONS REPORT. That bitch abandoned us." Sean was drunk as he paced Richard's small living room with a beer in his hand. "No fucking warning. I come back from a goddamn year of freaking hell and my wife's disappeared."

"Now I know why she left you." Richard looked on with repugnance as Sean's lubricated anger simmered and boiled. "Sean, get outta here, man. The kids are in bed, Louise has to work tomorrow. I refuse to argue with you. You've had too much to drink."

"I'm not finished." Sean turned bleary, red-rimmed eyes on his brother-in-law. "Why didn't you stop her?"

Richard stared at him and stood up. "You and I both know you sent her to hospital more than once. I'm glad I helped her get away from you. You need help, Sean."

Sean ignored him. "You're her brother. You could have stopped her, taken the keys, locked her in a room."

"Go home, Sean. We can't solve anything tonight. But, I promise you this. You'll never hit her again if I can help it." Richard walked to the front door and opened it. As Sean lurched forward, Richard relieved him of the half-empty can.

"Gimme that. I'm not finished yet."

"You're finished. Go walk it off." Richard manhandled Sean out the door, closed it and locked it. He walked back to the living room to turn off lights. Glancing out the window from the darkened room, he watched Sean stagger down the street. *I understand now, Andrea. Stay safe. Stay away.*

CHAPTER THREE

"IT'S SO LARGE AND BRIGHT. And look at the hardwood." Andrea's eyes widened with appreciation as she stepped into the sun-washed apartment. "The smells from the bakery make it feel so homey."

"Go explore. We can stay as long as we want. Neil is a friend." Flynn smiled at Andrea and grinned at Carol. "Isn't it special?"

Moments later, Andrea emerged from the smallest bedroom. "There's lots of closet space in all three bedrooms. I can easily fit Emily and Simon's clothes and toys in. And the master bedroom is almost elegant. It's more bedroom than I've had in my life."

"What do you think of the furniture?" Flynn ran his hand over an antique tea wagon. "I'd suggest several pieces would need to go into storage with young ones on the run."

"I'm not into antiques. I need solid, practical furniture that can be washed down or vacuumed." Andrea walked into the compact kitchen and nodded approvingly at the eating area, with its drop-leaf table and set of four chairs. "Everything in here is fine. The kids could do coloring at the table while I'm getting dinner ready."

"There's a deck out back and a small yard." Carol opened a door off the kitchen and beckoned them over. "It's shaded and low maintenance. Perfect for the kids."

"You sound like an agent." Flynn grinned at his business partner. "Selling the apartment's features."

"It sells itself." Carol chuckled. "What do you think, Andrea?"

"I think Flynn just found me a new home." Andrea grinned at them both, her eyes sparkling with pleasure. "Now we need to get me to a bank and start things happening so I can pay the rent."

"I'll take you over to the bank and introduce you. Flynn has to get back to the store, don't you?" Carol tried to look stern but broke into a grin.

"Yes, boss." Flynn winked at Andrea. "I actually let Carol buy into my store. Now she thinks she's the boss. I find it best to indulge her, to keep the peace."

Carol laughed out loud. "We take turns bossing each other, I think."

"You're right, actually." Flynn patted Andrea on the shoulder. "You two go on. I'm thrilled that you like it, Andrea. I'll tell Neil it's taken. You and I can come back this weekend with him, so you can tell him what to put in storage. It's Carol's turn to work the weekend shift."

"ERIN COPLAND, I'D LIKE YOU TO MEET MY FRIEND ANDREA GARRETT. She's moving into the area and needs to do some banking with you."

"Andrea, pleased to meet you." Erin put out his hand. At over six feet, he towered over his new client. "Did you win or lose the fight?"

Carol could see Andrea's flustered expression. "She had a close encounter with the ditch at the end of our driveway. Her car is a write-off."

"Sorry to hear that, Andrea. How can we help you?" Erin asked.

"I need to open checking, savings and investment accounts and transfer funds from my bank in New Jersey. I also need to apply for a credit card."

"Let's sit down, shall we?" He motioned her to a chair in front of his desk.

"I'll leave you two to get Andrea organized," Carol said. "I'll be out near the car somewhere." Carol let herself out and closed the door behind her. Andrea settled in a chair across from Erin.

"What brings you to Laskin?"

Andrea chuckled. "Seems fate brought me here. I was on my way to Boston and landed in a ditch. Carol found me and adopted me. Now she's convinced me to stay."

"I'm sure it didn't take much convincing. Laskin is a very pretty town and the community is very close knit, as I'm sure you'll discover." Erin smiled. "How about we get down to business?

Don't want to keep Carol waiting."

"I'll need to get some particulars." He opened a new client spreadsheet on his computer. "Your address?"

Andrea looked mildly flustered. "I'm staying with Carol and Devin at the moment, but I've found an apartment here in town." She gave him the address.

"When would you be moving in?"

"It's unoccupied and mostly furnished. I would think I could move in almost immediately."

"If that's the case, let's use that address. It'll save changing everything later."

Andrea glanced around the small modern office as he entered the information. A colorful landscape painting adorned one wall.

"Is that painting by a local artist?" she asked.

Erin looked up and nodded. "Yes. The bank buys from a variety of artists in the area. We usually donate at least one a year to a local fundraising event, as well."

"What a great idea." Andrea relaxed into the chair and looked out the window. What little traffic there was, went by slowly. She saw a couple of people stop to talk to each other, while another waved to them and crossed over to join them. *This is definitely my speed. I'm so glad I came here.*

After taking down all the information to open the accounts, Erin asked for Andrea's New Jersey bank information.

Andrea brought some papers out of her shoulder bag. "All of the information you need should be here. I want to transfer fifty thousand to start."

"This shouldn't take more than three or four working days. The money should be in your account by the middle of next week at the latest. Will you be depositing any money today?"

Andrea drew out an envelope and counted off some bills. "I'd like to deposit this please. I need to give the landlord a check for first and last month's rent and issue a check to get my Massachusetts driver's license."

Erin took the money and pulled out a deposit slip. "Here are ten checks to get you started. Once you have access, you can order more online. I'll set you up with an ATM card momentarily. Be sure to register your change of address with the post office. It's just a few doors down from here if you go left out the doors."

"Thanks very much, Erin. I really appreciate your help with all this." Andrea stood to shake his hand.

Erin stood. "You moving here with family?"

Andrea blinked at the surprise question. "I'm hoping my children will be joining me very shortly."

"None of my business, but not your husband?"

Andrea pulled herself up to her full height and spoke the words for the first time. "No, I'm getting a divorce."

"IT'S GOING TO TAKE A WHILE before I can get my Massachusetts driver's license." Andrea and Carol sat in the restaurant dining room behind the bakery's store front. "I have my proof of birth and proof of signature, but I need proof of residency and a cleared check for the fees. Erin said the funds transfer won't happen until next week."

"How's your cash situation?" Carol broke a large chocolate chip cookie in half and offered the other half to Andrea.

"I have enough to pay the first and last month rent plus the security deposit and still have enough for any other expenses until the bank transfer happens. I made sure I had enough cash with me to live on for three months, including buying new clothes and shoes."

"Tell you what. Get your Tricare claim paid and then we'll settle the hospital bill. Do you have enough to buy a used van?" Carol nibbled on her piece of cookie.

"No. But, once the transfer takes place I'll be fine, if you don't mind chauffeuring me around a few more days."

"On one condition."

"What's that?"

"We take off to Boston tomorrow and do some serious retail therapy. I'm buying lunch."

Andrea smiled brightly.

Carol watched her face transform. "I think that's the first time

I've seen your eyes really sparkle. See, told you retail therapy is good for the soul."

"You have no idea how long I've looked forward to being a self-determining person again. Even when Sean was overseas, he wanted reports on everything and how every dollar was spent."

"Does he know about your inheritance?"

"He knows there's some money for the kids' college funds. He doesn't know how much though."

"How did you hide that from him?"

"I left all the papers with Richard for safekeeping. It's almost as if I knew I would need it some day." Andrea chewed thoughtfully on some of the moist cookie. "This is incredibly decadent."

"I know. But we're responsible cookie monsters. We're only eating half each."

"The way I've been eating since I got here, it would be a wonder if any of my old clothes fit. I haven't worked out once and haven't chased children for the better part of a week. I'm going to be out of shape at this rate."

"Come riding with us in the morning. It's more of a workout than most people realize, especially for the abdominals." Carol finished the last of the cookie and wiped her fingers on a napkin.

"Seriously? I had no idea."

"Ride for an hour tomorrow morning. You'll know it the next day."

"I'll set the alarm. What time?"

"Six sharp at the paddock. Shower after, then breakfast."

"Sounds like I've been missing half the morning sleeping in until eight."

"You have. If you want to be a country girl, you need to get into the pattern of the animals. Up at dawn and sleeping at dusk."

"My dad used to say that, too. Okay, I'll be up with the birds tomorrow."

THEY WERE JUST COMING OUT OF THE BAKERY when Carol flagged down the veterinarian. "Val, this is Andrea Garrett. Andrea, meet Val."

Carol introduced Andrea to a solidly built woman with a thick blonde braid part-way down her back. "There's something you need to know about Andrea."

"Other than it looks like she went a round with a champion boxer and couldn't dodge his left hook?" Valerie McCormick was only a head taller than Andrea but easily twice her girth.

"You figured that out fast," Carol chuckled. "Andrea introduced herself to the horses today. Gregory is convinced she's a horse whisperer. She had Aero following her around like a puppy within minutes of meeting him."

Andrea's eyes widened as Carol described her first encounter with the horses. "Me, a horse whisperer? I'm just good with animals."

Val chortled and took a closer look at Andrea. "I've known those horses since Devin bought them. You couldn't get Aero to follow you on first meeting unless Gregory is right. That man knows horses. Aero thinks he's a king."

Andrea gazed in wonder at the two smiling women. "I've always loved animals, all animals. My father never worried about me doing anything to upset any of his patients, as he called them. He always knew I could settle them, whether they were frightened or in pain."

Val nodded her head at Carol and then looked at Andrea. "I've been looking for an assistant for a good year. I'd say I've found one."

"But what about my degree and doing an interview or a background check?"

"If Gregory says you're a horse whisperer, that's all I need to know. That Veterinary Technology degree is a big bonus though." Val stretched out her thick calloused hand. "And, you just told me everything I need to know about you. Can't pay you a city salary, but it'll be enough for a decent life in Laskin."

"I'm taking her to Boston to get some new clothes tomorrow and maybe see my former divorce lawyer. You can have her on Monday, but you have to come and pick her up. She doesn't have a vehicle yet."

"Heard about your close encounter with a ditch. Pretty hard on the front end." Val waved at someone driving by. "Car's a write-off?"

"Yes. I'm going to find a used van. I have two young children I hope to get custody of and bring here to live." Andrea watched for Val's reaction.

"I know a few women who take care of children while their parents work. I'll give you their names when the time comes. And I might know someone with a used van you could get pretty cheap."

"Thank you, Val." Andrea smiled. "Devin said there are lots of people around here who care about strangers. He's so right."

"You'll be helping someone yourself one of these days. That's the way it's supposed to work."

"I couldn't agree with you more."

"We'll get along just fine." Val hugged Carol and gave Andrea a pat on the shoulder. "I need to get going. I'll pick you up Monday at eight. I'm easing up a bit these days."

"Eight it is. It'll give me time to go riding with Carol and Devin."

Carol and Andrea waved as Val drove away in her pickup. "Let's see, you found an apartment, got set up with the bank and landed a job. Plus you might have a lead on daycare and a van. Not bad for one day. I can only imagine what we'll accomplish tomorrow in Boston."

"If our shopping goes as well as all this went today, we'll be finished before lunch."

"The shopping gods always smile on me," Carol said, with a grin. "We may have to stay overnight. You ever been to Boston?"

"I was there for a holiday weekend with my parents when I was about fifteen. I loved it. I think that's why I wanted to move there. We had a great time that weekend."

"It's changed a lot in some ways since you were there, but in other ways it hasn't changed a bit. There's still that New England charm, especially in early spring when everything is fresh and new."

"Right now, I feel my whole life is fresh and new. I haven't felt like this since I first went away to university and had my whole future ahead of me."

CAROL LOOKED AT DEVIN AND FLYNN working beside each other in their state-of-the art kitchen. "Do you believe my good fortune, Andrea? I not only married an accomplished chef but his manager's partner is also an amazing cook."

"How do you all stay so slim with all this fine food?" Andrea patted her tummy. "I've been so spoiled. Once the kids are here, it's back to Cheerios and peanut butter."

Flynn looked up from where he was laying out rice paper wrappers. "With the bakery next door, I'm sure Emily and Simon will expand their culinary repertoire quickly. No Cheerio can beat the smell of a fresh chocolate chip croissant."

"Good point, Flynn." Andrea grinned. "And they love muffins and bagels."

"Is there anything we need while we're in Boston tomorrow?" Carol threw the question out.

Devin set down his knife next to a mound of finely chopped vegetables. "I could go in with you. I need to check in with one of the engineers on a new project. You could drop me off."

"How about we stay overnight and show Andrea around a bit?" Carol winked at Andrea. "You could take us out for dinner. Maybe Jennifer and Ben could meet up with us?"

"Sounds like a great idea. The cleaning service went in today so the house will be all set."

"You have a house in Boston?" Andrea's eyes widened. "I thought you only had this farm."

"At one point, Carol and I had four properties between us." Devin grinned and rolled his eyes. "We each had a condo, I had the farm, and then I inherited a charming Victorian from a dear friend."

"How did you keep track of where things were? It was always hard for me to remember because we moved around a lot. But we only lived in one house or apartment at a time. I can't imagine rotating among four."

Devin chuckled. "It didn't last long. Carol sold first. We had the Victorian extensively renovated after a fire. Once that was done, I sold my condo. We were down to two properties within a year, give or take."

"Would anyone like a glass of wine before dinner?" Carol looked at Andrea. "How's your head? Think you could have a glass?"

Andrea took a deep breath and smiled. "I feel fine now. And this is a day to celebrate at least one of our many accomplishments."

"Andrea starts working for Val on Monday. The minute I told her about Gregory saying she's a horse whisperer, Val was hooked."

Devin and Flynn looked at each other in mutual astonishment. Devin spoke first. "What do you mean, Andrea's a horse whisperer?"

"I mean dear, she had Aero following her around like a puppy not five minutes after walking into the paddock. All three of them. Didn't Gregory tell you?"

"He's over at the Sheridan farm helping with the lambing. Probably won't see him until tomorrow." Flynn spooned the vegetable mixture into the wrappers, rolled them and sealed the ends. A deep fryer stood ready on the counter.

"Aero followed Andrea? He only does that with me. He doesn't even follow Gregory. It's like he knows Gregory is his hired help."

"A horse whisperer. Wait until the word gets around." Flynn went over to stir a pot of fragrant Pho Bo soup. "You'll be bringing in your own business in no time."

Andrea smiled happily and sipped her wine. "That would be wonderful. I feel so alive when I'm around animals. I've really missed them the past few years."

SEAN LOOKED AROUND THE COMPACT KITCHEN. It was a mess of dirty dishes, empty takeout and an overflowing trash bin. He walked to the fridge, opened the door and surveyed the contents. There was little apart from the beer he'd bought. *The bitch planned this,* he fumed. He picked one up and pulled the tab just as the phone rang.

"Sean Garrett?"

He snarled. "Who wants to know?"

"This is the Massachusetts State Trooper's office."

Sean frowned and put the beer down. He ran a hand over his blonde buzz cut. "Did you find my wife?"

"No, sir. But we can confirm that she was in a single vehicle collision on the night of April eighteenth about an hour and a half outside Boston. She was taken to St. Luke's hospital with head injuries. It is unknown where she went after being discharged."

"And her car?"

"Unknown, sir. It was left in the ditch. We have no record of it after the accident and no report of it still being there."

"Do you have any information on her whereabouts now? With the head injuries, I'm worried she may have amnesia. Our children want their mommy to come home." Sean's eyes were hard and cold as he picked up the beer and took a long pull.

"We have no information, sir. There was no crime and no property damage. No charges were laid."

"Thank you, officer. Where did you say the accident happened?" Sean wrote the location on a piece of paper, thanked the officer, hung up, picked up his beer and got another one from the fridge.

Walking into the living room, he sat down in his favorite chair and looked over to Andrea's empty one; it was next to a basket that had once held children's books and colorful magazines. "I'm coming to bring you home where you belong, Andrea. You can run, but you can't hide. I will find you. Bet on it, bitch."

CHAPTER FOUR

ANDREA STRETCHED AND LOOKED AT THE CLOCK. *Almost time to get ready for the big trip to the city,* she mused. *But first, a brisk ride on Pablo.*

Turning back the covers she hopped out of bed and went to open the curtains. The sun was just beginning to peek over the horizon as she pulled them back. Looking at the pastoral scene before her, she thought about her babies and felt the tears well up.

Just a few more days and they'll be in my arms again. She folded her arms across her breasts and lay her head on her shoulder. She could almost smell Simon's hair after his bath. Stretching her neck, she smiled, remembering a giggling embrace from Emily, her chubby arms wrapped around her neck as they rubbed noses.

I have to do this carefully and legally. She went back to make the bed. *Richard and Louise will take good care of them. Sean won't take care of them alone.*

Andrea shivered in the cool room as she thought of Sean's anger at her actually getting away from him. She pulled on a soft, aqua sweater and loose jeans. As she stood brushing her hair, she thought, *I'm so glad I finally left him.*

"WHAT'S YOUR BUDGET FOR CLOTHES?" Carol turned her head back to look at Andrea as she finished texting her brother.

"I figure I can get away with about five hundred dollars, including some good work boots. If I'm going to be around farmyards, I'll need two or three pair of jeans, too."

"I have some we could shorten for you. I have way more clothes than any one woman could wear."

Devin kept his eyes on the traffic and grinned. "You finally admit it. You still have unopened boxes in one of the spare bedrooms."

"I forgot about those. I don't even remember what's in them."
Carol looked out at the looming skyline of Boston. On this sunny
spring day, the city seemed to sparkle. Carol's phone chirped.
"Carol Brock here… Hi, Peter. Good to hear from you. How's
your schedule today? … because I have a new client for you." She
listened. "Perfect. We'll see you at three o'clock sharp.

"You now have an appointment with one of the best divorce
lawyers in Massachusetts."

Andrea grinned. "Guess I'll need a nice outfit to wear. Time to
shop."

"PETER STINSON, MEET ANDREA GARRETT. Ms. Garrett needs
your help to get a divorce and gain custody of her two children."

"Hello, Andrea." The aging lawyer shook hands with both
women. "Did you want Carol to come in with you or stay out here?"

Andrea looked at Carol. "If you don't mind, Carol, I'd like you
to stay."

"I don't mind at all."

"Then let's all go into my office and have a chat." He led the
women down a bright hall past elegantly framed oil paintings of
long-dead partners. "How are you doing, Carol? How's Devin?"

"We both love living at the farm almost full-time, especially at
this time of year."

"Any news of your ex?"

"Remarried and produced another child at the age of fifty.
He'll be a senior citizen just when his daughter gets into her teens."
Carol smirked. "He won't know what hit him. Talk about payback."

Peter laughed. "I'm enjoying my grandchildren, all four of them.
But they go home at the end of the day. By then, I'm exhausted."

ANDREA FELT MORE IN CONTROL WHEN THEY EMERGED from the
lawyer's office an hour later. "Thank you for introducing me to
Peter. He's such a sweet man."

"To you, yes. With Sean, it will be an entirely different story.
Peter is no soft touch. He'll go for the jugular with Sean over the
abuse." Carol eased her BMW into the rush hour gridlock. "Let's

go pick up Devin and stop by the house to freshen up. We're meeting Jennifer and Ben at six."

"Flynn told me about them. Jennifer is your best friend, isn't she?" Andrea smoothed her hands over new black slacks, which were paired with a silver grey tailored shirt and a short-waisted bomber jacket.

"She is. She stood by me as my real estate career unraveled because of a con artist boyfriend and, less than a year later, a psychopathic client who had once been Devin's girlfriend." They pulled up in front of Devin's office. "People I thought were my friends abandoned me in droves. Jennifer and Ben stuck by me.

"I know you'll like Jennifer. And Ben is very special, too. He was a Pulitzer prize-winning journalist. His alma mater is the same as Ashley's. She thinks he walks on water." Carol waited as Devin climbed into the back seat.

"I've seen him on TV many times. He always seemed to be at the center of the action." Andrea reached up to finger the dangling earrings that Carol insisted on buying for her.

"Hi, you. How'd it go?" Carol blew a kiss to Devin as he buckled up. She set off in the direction of their Boston home.

"We're on track to start the Henderson homestead project within a month if we can get the permits lined up. I think Mrs. Henderson will be very pleased with our plans. And we're right within her budget." Devin stretched his long legs as far as he could in the back seat of the compact BMW. "How did things go for you, ladies?"

"We scored a number of major coups in the clothing and footwear departments. The trunk is pretty well full. Andrea is now the proud owner of a fine pair of steel-toed boots."

"What would you need steel-toed boots for?"

"Ever had a pregnant sow step on your toes?" Andrea laughed. "Not all animals are quite as agile as the horses. I learned that the hard way."

"JENNIFER, BEN." CAROL STROLLED OVER to where her friends were already seated in one of their favorite restaurants and gave both warm hugs. "I'd like to introduce you to our new friend,

Andrea Garrett. Andrea is staying with us for a while until she moves into her own place in Laskin."

"Hello, Andrea. Good to meet you." Jennifer put out her hand. "Carol emailed me about your situation. I don't know if she told you, I'm a retired social worker. If you need any help navigating the system, I can help."

"I'll definitely keep that in mind. I don't know the rules for Massachusetts. I've been doing online research, but someone who knows the system could definitely be a help."

Conversation was put on hold as a waitress stopped by to take drink orders.

Jennifer looked over to where her silver-haired husband was in animated conversation with Devin and Carol. "Carol mentioned that your husband may have post-traumatic stress disorder. Ben has PTSD. He was a journalist covering Afghanistan and all the Middle East hotspots for close to twenty years. We've talked a lot about it. He feels he has it under control now, and he was never violent in any way."

"My husband is a warrior. He likes to fight and kill people. For him, there will always be a war he needs to fight, even if it's at home. It's why I left him. I was beginning to develop symptoms of PTSD myself. For the sake of my children, I just couldn't come undone." Jennifer abruptly stopped talking. "This is amazing. How did we get to this level of discussion so fast?"

Jennifer chuckled and patted Andrea's hand. "Carol says you're a horse whisperer. Well, I'm a people whisperer."

Andrea looked at her and smiled. "Now I know what Aero, Sabrina and Pablo experienced. I guess I knew instinctively you would understand."

Later, as they sipped on their drinks, Ben turned to Andrea. "From what Carol tells me, your husband's abuse pre-dates his PTSD."

"It does. He told me he was a very effective tight end in football in high school and college. Seems he took a few too many tackles. It was very noticeable when he'd been drinking. He'd lose his balance easily." Andrea sipped her Shiraz. "I think whatever his overseas experiences were just amplified the effects of his brain injuries and his violent tendencies. I don't blame the army or the war. From what I've seen, he went in with problems. But he's in now with many more problems and that's what I can't handle."

"Are you getting any support from the military?"

"We'll see. Carol introduced me to her divorce lawyer. We met him this afternoon. He's going to do the paperwork to file for divorce. He's requesting for me to have full custody of my children on the basis of an unpredictably violent home environment. He's pretty confident we'll get them. I have witnesses going back over three years, plus medical records."

"I don't mean to pry, but *medical records*?" Jennifer glanced over at Ben.

"He dislocated my shoulder when I was pregnant with Emily. I knew the base doctor didn't buy my story about falling, but he didn't say anything." Andrea paused as they gave their dinner orders.

"Another time I was treated for second degree burns on my arm. There were some other injuries as well. It's documented." Andrea looked at them. "I'd rather not talk about it right now, if you don't mind."

Ben cleared his throat. "When I was covering Afghanistan and Iraq, I met a lot of guys who talked about how much they missed their wives and families and then told me that they were on their fourth or fifth mission.

"I interviewed several for a documentary about life in the field. They told me that they'd go back to the real world and within weeks, start thinking about when they could get back. I was the same way for almost twenty years. It gets in your blood. Real life just isn't exiting enough."

Andrea nodded. "I think for Sean, real life is never exciting enough. Marrying me and having a family was Sean doing what he thought he *should* do so he could be part of the military family."

"There's such a strong culture of unit solidarity. I saw that all the time overseas. These guys have each other's backs." Ben sipped his drink.

Andrea nodded again. "Exactly. And it's the same when they get back home, from what I can tell, especially when it comes to covering up for abusers. I know of one woman who was slapped around by her husband in front of four of his buddies. They didn't do a thing to stop it." Andrea felt tears welling up and swallowed as her throat tightened.

At the arrival of their dinners, Andrea smiled and chuckled. "I can't think of the last time I went out to an adults-only dinner. Even when I go out with other people, I end up sharing my meal with Emily or holding Simon when I'm trying to eat. This is such a treat."

"Enjoy." Carol patted Andrea's arm. "Every mom deserves some adult time. This is it."

"For just this one night, I'm not going to feel guilty about being in Boston and having dinner out without my children."

"Atta girl." Ben raised his glass. "Here's to one adult-only dinner. Much as I love our three grandchildren, it's good to get away once in a while with just the adults."

"We wouldn't know about that, would we Devin?" Carol raised her glass and smiled.

"And won't for a while, I'm sure."

"Ah, but you forget that we have adopted Andrea. We are now honorary grandparents."

Andrea beamed at both of them and raised her glass. "I can't imagine a better pair of grandparents, honorary or not. You two are helping me change my life for the better. Here's to you, Carol and Devin."

CHAPTER FIVE

SEAN CLIMBED OUT OF HIS PICKUP and walked over to the paddock. The warm moist air was a shock from the air conditioning.

"Excuse me, sir. I'm trying to locate a woman who was in a car accident a week ago. Troopers told me it happened at the end of your driveway."

"Wouldn't know much about it. I just work here. And, I've been working over at another farm." Gregory looked over from grooming Aero.

"So you know there was an accident."

"Heard about it."

"Did you see the driver? She's my wife. She's disappeared." Sean tried not to let his frustration show.

"I saw her, yes. Don't know where she is now."

Sean looked hard at the man. "When did you last see her? Was she here?"

"Saw her when they towed her car away. If you'll excuse me, I have chores."

"Damn it, I'm trying to find my wife, the mother of my children. Why won't you help me?" He pulled off his cap and ran his hand over his head and put the cap back on.

Gregory turned Aero loose in the paddock and walked over to the fence. "Look mister, I mind my own business. I told you, I don't know where your wife is. Now, please leave. I have to work."

Gregory watched as Sean strode back to his truck, got in and slammed his door. Once the truck was well down the lane, he pulled out his cell phone. "Better spread the word around Laskin, Flynn. Andrea's husband is here looking for her."

Flynn hung up the antique phone on the wall. "So, Andrea's big bad husband is trying to find her. We'll just see about that, won't we?" He spoke to a cherubic Hummel figurine on the shelf above his head. "I'll see you later, sweetie. Time to make a few phone calls."

SEAN LOOKED ALL OVER THE YARD as he pulled in to the local garage. He parked his truck in the only slice of shade on the lot. "Hello? Anyone here?" He aimed for the open bay door.

"What can I do for you?" Casey McCormick backed away from the engine he was working on and pulled up to his full height. He grabbed a rag from his back pocket to wipe his hands.

"Name's Sean Garrett, sir." Sean put out his hand.

"Better not. Hand's real greasy, son." Casey's face was neutral. "What can I do for you?"

"I'm looking for my wife's car. She was in an accident near here last week and I thought maybe it was towed here for repairs."

"What's your wife's name?"

"Andrea Garrett."

"I don't have a client by that name. She hasn't been here."

"Where else could her car have been taken then?"

"I'm the only mechanic around here. There are several salvage yards in the area. Might want to check with them."

"Thank you, sir. I'll do that."

As the pickup pulled away, Casey walked into his cramped waiting area and reached over the counter for the phone. "Hi hon. Andrea's husband was just here looking for her. I'm gonna call around to the yards and warn them. You better spread the word in town."

IT WAS NOON, AND SEAN WAS GETTING NOWHERE. Driving along the main street, he saw the Sweet Repose Bakery and Tea Room and decided to stop. He threw his cap on the seat and ran a hand over his head.

Getting out of the pickup, he took a moment to look around and noticed a For Rent sign being taken out of the window of the house next to the bakery. Tempting aromas drew him through the bakery's front door.

"Good afternoon, sir. Welcome to the Sweet Repose. Would you like a table?"

"Sure. Sounds good." He noted the case full of treats of all kinds. "Those look great. Haven't had any home-baked desserts in months."

"You'll have to get some on the way out. My name is Eric Lesage and that's my wife Sheila behind the counter."

"Hi. My name is Sean Garrett. Just down from Newark." Sean didn't notice the sparkle in Eric's eyes give way to instant hardness.

"Right this way, Mr. Garrett." He brought him to a corner table next to a window and put a menu down. "Today's soup is cream of broccoli. The special is chicken parmesan. I'll be back with some water. Would you like something to drink?

"I'll have a Bud, thanks."

Eric walked smartly to the storefront and took his wife aside. "That's Andrea Garrett's husband. Call in the troops. And don't serve up his meal too quickly. I want everyone to have time to get here."

Eric took a can of beer from the cooler, picked up a tall glass and walked slowly back to the table. "Here you go, Mr. Garrett. I'll come back in a few minutes for your order." He poured half the glass and put both on the table.

Sean downed the half glass and emptied the rest of the can into it. "Better bring me another."

When Eric returned, Sean had a photo of Andrea on the table. "You seen my wife over the past week? She was in an accident and seems to have disappeared."

Eric picked up the photo and looked at it closely. "Doesn't look like anyone I've seen around here." The smiling beauty in the photo didn't look like the Andrea he'd met.

"So, what would you like to order?" Eric put the photo down.

"I'll have the special."

"With or without the soup?"

"With the soup."

"Thank you. I'll be back with some fresh-baked bread in a couple of minutes. It's just warming up now."

Eric returned to the front just as Valerie and Casey McCormick walked in, setting the bells over the door ringing.

"C'mon in folks. Haven't seen you in here for lunch in a long time."

"Today is special." Val winked at Eric. "Gregory and Flynn are on their way, too."

Sheila walked up to the counter. "Hello, you two. Nice to get you together for lunch. Just spoke to Erin Copland. He's on his way. And so is Neil, Andrea's landlord. He was none too happy when he found out why Andrea is moving here."

In less than half an hour, the Sweet Repose restaurant area filled. Looking around, Sean realized everyone knew each other. When his soup arrived, he ordered a third beer. He didn't notice Eric's sly smile or the wink he sent Val.

"How's your lunch?" Eric stopped by when he noticed Sean's beer glass was empty. "Can I bring you another beer?"

"Lunch is fine. Yeah, I'll have another beer, thanks."

Val looked at her husband. "Think it's about time, dear?"

"Let him work through that beer. We want him completely over the legal limit when he drives away. Eric has the troopers lined up at both ends of town."

SEAN HAD JUST FINISHED HIS FOURTH BEER WHEN HE LOOKED UP and saw a stocky woman approach his table, followed by the town mechanic. He had a good buzz on and smiled at them. "Hello again, sir."

He made to stand up but changed his mind and sat down abruptly. "Is this your lovely wife?"

Val snorted. "You've had one too many beers if you think I'm lovely."

Sean grinned up at her until he saw the look on her face.

"You've been asking around about Andrea Garrett."

He swallowed uncomfortably when he realized that the restaurant was suddenly quiet.

"She's my wife. She was in an accident. I want to find her and bring her home."

"She doesn't want to go home. We know all about you, Mister Garrett. In this town, we don't truck with people beating their women and terrifying their children." As she said the words, everyone in the restaurant stood up. Eric and Sheila came over and stood with Val and Casey.

"You'd best leave now, Mister Garrett. Your money is no good here."

Sean looked around him and stood unsteadily. "I ain't finished with Andrea."

"You are in *this* town." Eric quietly escorted him to the door and watched while he climbed into his truck. "Call the troopers. He's heading north."

"HELLO OFFICER." SEAN NERVOUSLY CHEWED SOME GUM as he lowered his window. "I wasn't speeding."

"I need you to step out of your vehicle, sir." Trooper First Class Elsie Vaughan stepped back as the smell of beer assailed her nose.

"I haven't done anything wrong. What's this about?" Sean crossed his arms over the steering wheel to prop himself up.

"Step out of your truck now, sir." She looked over at the unmarked patrol car and nodded.

Sean opened the door and stepped out. He stumbled a bit but righted himself and stood up straight.

"Driver's license and car registration, please."

He pulled out his wallet and handed over the license. "The registration is in the glove compartment."

Trooper Vaughan was joined by a colleague.

"He's DUI for sure. Got a good ten minutes on video."

"Hey, I only had a couple of beers for lunch." Sean found it a bit difficult to focus on the pretty trooper. "Don't you folks have something better to do than harass an off-duty soldier?"

"Come with me to the squad car, sir. I want you to take a breathalyzer test."

"What if I don't want to?"

"Then you'll lose your license for a lot longer than if you do."

Trooper Vaughan and her colleague guided Sean.

"You know, you'd be really pretty if you smiled."

"Arresting people who are DUI is not something I smile about. I've seen too many people killed or maimed by people like you."

Sean fell silent. *This day is going to hell in a hand basket,* he thought.

CHAPTER SIX

"YOU WON'T BELIEVE WHAT'S BEEN GOING ON BACK HOME," Carol said, putting her iPhone down. "Sean Garrett is cooling his heels in jail as we speak."

"What?" Andrea looked up from her own iPhone and stopped texting Richard. "What happened?"

"Seems Sean came looking for you, my dear. He asked around and then went to the Sweet Repose for lunch. Thanks to Flynn and Gregory, about twenty people we know decided to have lunch there too, including Val and her husband Casey, the town mechanic. Eric made sure Sean had plenty of time to drink as many beers as he wanted and then they ran him out of town—right into the hands of the state troopers. He's been arrested for DUI."

"Wonder what will happen to him? He's had two convictions in New Jersey. I usually did all the driving if I knew he'd have access to alcohol."

"Well, you weren't around to save him today. You realize he was right beside your apartment?"

Andrea shuddered. "I don't ever want him to know where I live."

"How about you text Richard? Maybe he could bring Emily and Simon down tomorrow? They can stay with us while you get the apartment set up."

"You sure you want a couple of small children under foot?"

"It's only for a few days, and yes, I'm sure." Carol smiled over at Devin. "Think you can handle it, big guy?"

"I have a way with children. Ask Jennifer and Ben's grandchildren." Devin gave a thumbs up. "Let's get these kids here where they can run around and get dirty. If they're lucky, they'll see Pasha's kittens."

"The heck with the long distance charge. I'm calling Richard right now."

Ten minutes later, she dropped her phone back in her purse and sighed. "I'm so glad I gave my brother a key to my house. He's offered to borrow a pickup, go get Emily's bed and Simon's crib and all their things and bring them all here tomorrow. He's going to pick everything up tonight after Louise gets home from work, so he can leave right after breakfast."

"Thank goodness you bought bedding and towels in Boston."

Andrea smiled as they came up the farm road. She could see Sabrina and Pablo in the paddock. "Where's Aero?"

"Gregory probably has him in the stable for something."

As they pulled up to the side of the house, Gregory emerged from the stable and walked over to the dusty BMW.

"I've got Aero in his stall. I think he may have a tick. He's been scratching up against the rails. Haven't found one yet."

Devin walked briskly towards the stable, with Carol and Andrea following. All three changed into rubber boots at the door.

Devin approached Aero quietly and reached out to pat down his nose. "What's up with my beautiful boy?" The horse snickered quietly and put his head forward. Devin saw the evidence of heavy rubbing near his flank.

Andrea looked on. "This could take a while. Depends what kind of tick it is. Some are no bigger than a poppy seed."

"Around here, it's usually moose ticks."

"Those are really hard to kill and at this time of year there would likely be several. Well, let's get to work and find the little buggers. Aero is not a happy horse at the moment. Has he had less energy than usual?"

Gregory crooked up his eyebrow. "Now that you mention it, yes."

"Moose ticks can cause anemia. He may have a mild case. Val will have some vitamins."

"FOUND THEM." ANDREA PEERED AROUND AERO'S HIND. "They're just under the top of his tail. He'd never be able to scratch that spot, poor fellow. I'll need a pair of tweezers plus a jar with some rubbing alcohol. Only way to kill these critters is to drown them in alcohol."

Devin and Carol were standing with their arms linked, watching Andrea and Gregory work together.

"I'll get them." Carol jogged back to the house.

"Come, have a look." Andrea motioned Devin to come over.

Devin stepped into the narrow stall and worked his way back to where Andrea had found some small brown buttons sticking out of Aero's coat. "I hadn't noticed this patch before. You, Gregory?"

"No. I'm sure I would have seen them at this size."

"These have probably been here for a few months but were too small to see. They look fully engorged now. They probably would have fallen off in a couple more days and you'd have a new colony to go after all the horses."

Carol returned with the tweezers and jar of alcohol. Andrea dipped the tweezers into the jar for a few seconds and then got to work.

"Okay Aero, I need you to stand very still while I get your little friends into a nice clean bath. Gregory, if you could hold the jar, please."

A few moments later, Andrea stepped back. "That looks like it. Just set the jar on a ledge somewhere for a few days. That'll be the end of that little family."

"I think Val's going to like your work style, Andrea." Devin smiled at her. "I know Aero does."

"Like I said, I've been around animals all my life until just the past few years. I'm doing what I've always loved to do."

"It shows."

"RICHARD JUST TEXTED THAT SEAN WILL GET OUT OF JAIL after his arraignment tomorrow. He's asked him to come and get him with a thousand dollars cash. That's the maximum fine, so it could be less. He's going to drop Emily and Simon here first, of course."

Andrea looked at Carol. "It makes me nervous having him so close by. Even though I know he's locked away, for now. And

Richard will make sure he gets home sober. I just want to hug my babies and start building a new life with them and for them."

"And that starts tomorrow. Let's check the cupboards and stock in the groceries we'll need with the children around." Carol started opening cabinet doors. "Then we can stop by Neil Shelby's with your first and last month rent and pick up the keys. Maybe go over and see what to keep and what he could store."

"That sounds like a plan, Carol. I need to keep busy. I'm so excited!" Andrea clapped her hands with delight. "I'll be holding Emily and Simon by lunch time tomorrow. I can hardly believe it."

"Ten days is a long time when you're a mother," Carol said.

"I've never been away from them for more than one night since they were born. This has been so rough. But, the end is in sight."

"NEIL SHELBY, MEET YOUR NEW TENANT, Andrea Garrett." Carol stood in a roomy country kitchen on the outskirts of town. Large windows overlooked a sloping field, with a border of trees along its edge. "I've always liked the view from here. Your great-grandfather picked a good location, for sure."

"Best view around." Neil looked at the two women and smiled.

"Good to meet you, Andrea. Met your husband yesterday. Very briefly. He seemed to be in a bit of a hurry to get out of town." The grizzled farmer had a sparkle in his eyes and a wide smirk.

"I heard that Sean didn't even stop to pay his bill," Andrea said. "I must settle with Sheila and Eric when we're over there later."

"They won't let you pay," he said. "We all agreed it was worth the price of admission to witness Val and Eric reading him the riot act. We left enough in tips to more than cover your ex's bill."

"Well, I still need to go and thank them, that's for sure. That was some phone tree you folks were working."

He chuckled. "I hear you have two little ones arriving soon. I still have a high chair in my shed if you want it."

"That would be great, thanks! They're arriving tomorrow." Andrea smiled into a face etched with deep wrinkles. "Somehow, I wouldn't have expected an offer of a high chair from you."

"Oh, I never get rid of anything," he said. "My late wife was always telling me to give things to the Goodwill. Now my daughter's saying the same thing. But I saved her a bundle when the element on her hot water tank went. I have several out back."

"I'll keep your supply shed in mind, if I need anything. You wouldn't happen to have a passenger van back there somewhere?"

"I don't, but I know who does. Didn't Val tell you?"

"She mentioned knowing someone who might be willing to sell me one cheaply. Why?"

Neil smiled. "It's Val and Casey's old van. They only use it to ferry church groups around. It's about fifteen years old, but Casey keeps it in perfect running shape."

It was Andrea's turn to chuckle. "I start working for Val on Monday. I'll have to use my charms and get her to sell it to me."

"Casey will thank you. He's the one who does all the driving. He told me once he never gets a day off. The shop is open six days a week, and Val always has some outing planned on his so-called day of rest."

"After what they've both done for me, they can name their price."

"How about we head to the apartment with my truck? There's a few pieces I'd like to take out. Family heirlooms my wife got tired of dusting. But, she'd have my hide if they were damaged by your little ones. She told me she'd come back from the grave to haunt me if anything happened to them."

"Then we'll get them out of there, for sure. When can I move in? I'm anxious to get settled into my new home."

"Here's the keys to the front and back doors. Let's get the high chair. If you see anything else you want, we'll load it up. You can move in any time. I know where you live."

AN HOUR LATER, THEY PULLED UP IN FRONT OF THE STATELY VICTORIAN DUPLEX with half a truckload of furniture, dishes, cutlery and pots and pans. Andrea grabbed a box and led the way. Setting it down, she unlocked the door and held it open for Carol and Neil, who followed with two more boxes.

"Welcome. You're my first visitors. I'd offer you some coffee, but I haven't been grocery shopping yet."

Andrea walked into the sunny apartment and took a box of dishes to the kitchen. "This is such a classic old kitchen. But, I'll need a ladder to reach the top shelves."

"Actually, there's a step ladder in the garden shed. The previous tenant was very tall." Neil put the old wooden high chair next to the kitchen table. Sunlight streaming in the window reflected generations of nicks and scratches in its still shiny surface.

They were all startled when the doorbell rang. Andrea went into the small vestibule and opened the door. "Oh my. Sheila, Eric, what a lovely surprise!"

The smell of fresh coffee and muffins wafted into the apartment, which was now filling with boxes. "Thought you might like an afternoon coffee break. A little welcome from your new neighbors."

"The best neighbors a girl like me could want, too. You should know I have a very sweet tooth."

"We're counting on it. Oh yes, here's a bag of fresh dinner rolls to bring back with you. Flynn is still trying to wheedle my grandmother's recipe out of me. Let him know I'm considering it now that he found you to be our neighbor." Sheila handed Andrea a large paper bag.

"Won't you come in?"

Eric laid a hand lovingly on his wife's shoulder. "Sheila, you stay and take a break. I'll watch over the store."

"Thank you, dear. I'm sure Andrea and Carol would like the lowdown on Sean's quick departure yesterday."

"We would," they said in unison as everyone burst out laughing.

"I DON'T KNOW ABOUT YOU, BUT I'M BUSHED." Andrea brought in the last bag of groceries and set it on the counter as Carol followed with a bag of potatoes. "I could move in with the kids tomorrow, you realize."

Carol crooked her head and shook it slowly. "Probably best to stay over with us at least one or two more nights. The bed and crib will need to be assembled. You'll still have all their clothes to unpack and put away, as well as their toys. I heard you telling Richard about the paintings and other things you want that came from your parents."

"You're right. Simon's never been through a move and Emily was barely walking the last time. Staying over with my brother and his wife is one thing. This is a major move."

"Take your time with them, Andrea. Maybe bring them here a couple of times to visit it and see that their toys and clothes are here. Bring them to Sweet Repose to pick something out. Let them settle in on their own terms."

"And I still need to find daycare. I'm hoping to find someone who can come here instead of me having to pack them up every day. And I need Val's van." Andrea emptied a bag onto the counter, opened all the cupboard doors and started putting jars and cans onto the empty shelves. "I think I'll need a few more days before making the final move."

"Good decision, my dear. Children are pretty resilient, but a lot is happening."

"I'm so lucky to have someone like you for support and good advice. It's the first time since I was married that I feel I have a real support network." Andrea went over and hugged Carol. "This is going to work. I can feel it."

"THEY'RE HERE!" ANDREA WATCHED FROM A WINDOW AS A LARGE DUSTY PICKUP lurched up the pot-holed drive towards the paddock. *I hope Richard's planning to go to a car wash before he brings back Jim's truck.*

She and Carol went into the mud room and slipped on Crocs as Devin and Gregory came out of the stable. Flynn arrived along the path from his house carrying a box with a covered dish in it.

"I'll just put this casserole on the counter and be right back to help."

"Flynn, that wasn't necessary. I just went grocery shopping." Andrea smiled fondly at her new friend.

"You can put it in the freezer for another day, sweetie. You won't have time or energy after working with Val all day. Trust me.

She puts in a long hard day at this time of year."

Flynn disappeared into the house as Richard stepped out of the truck. Andrea ran to the passenger side and peered in. Both Emily and Simon were asleep in their car seats. Carol came over to look in.

"Oh my, Andrea. They're adorable."

"They can both be little hellions when they're awake. But like this, they're angels."

"Let's leave them and get out what they'll need for the next few days. We'll take the rest over to your apartment after Richard has a few minutes to catch his breath."

The two women went to the back of the pickup and started opening boxes.

"Too bad Louise wasn't there to help. This packing is pretty haphazard." Andrea smiled and looked over to where her brother was chatting with the other men. "But he pulled this together on no notice. Gotta love him for that."

They were interrupted by a whimpering cry that escalated as Simon awoke and found himself in strange surroundings. Andrea felt a tug in her heart at the familiar sound. "Hello, Simon. It's Mommy, my big boy. Let's get you and Emily out of the truck. They have kittens here. Would you like to see some kittens?"

Simon put his thumb in his mouth sleepily but reached out both arms when Andrea unbuckled him and leaned in to bring him out. Cuddling him in close, she breathed in his warm scent.

Flynn came out and walked over to the pickup. "And who is this handsome young man?"

"This is Simon." Andrea eased Simon's thumb out of his mouth and kissed his chubby hand. "Simon, this is Flynn. He's my friend. He knows where we can get the best chocolate chip cookies ever made. Isn't that right, Flynn?"

"It is. And we just happen to have some of those cookies in the kitchen. Do you think Simon would like one?"

"Would you like a cookie, Simon?"

Simon nodded his head against his mother's chest and gave Flynn a shy look.

"Mommy!" Andrea turned to see Emily reaching her arms out to her. She handed Simon into Flynn's arms and reached down to plant a kiss on her daughter's forehead.

"Look at you. You've grown since I went away. I bet your clothes hardly fit." Andrea unbuckled Emily and swooped her down to the ground. "Where's my hug?"

Emily launched herself into her mother's open arms and wrapped her legs around her waist. "Uncle Richard says there's a cat here and she has kittens. I want to see the kittens, Mommy."

"Let's get you a little snack, and then we'll find the kittens. I have to find your boots before we can go in the stable. It's pretty dirty back there for your pretty shoes."

Carol squatted in front of Emily. "Hi Emily. I'm Carol. I have three horses. Do you like horses?"

Emily looked at Carol wide-eyed. "You have horses? They're pretty."

"They're also very big. Wait until you see them. They're so tall you'll have to sit on your uncle's shoulder to touch their heads. How about we find those cookies while your mom finds your boots? Want to see my house?"

Emily danced away holding Carol's hand.

Richard excused himself and went over to where Andrea was peering into box after box.

"Do you know where their rain boots are? They really want to go in the stable."

Richard looked over the array of boxes and homed in on a large one. He pulled open the flaps. "Yep, this is the box of shoes and boots. I put a bunch of yours in there, too."

"You shouldn't have, but thanks. I bought everything I need in Boston, yesterday."

"Louise always says women can never have enough shoes. So, when I saw these, I figured you'd need them."

"How about a big hug from your little sister?" Andrea smiled and put her arms up around his broad shoulders. "Thank you so much for canceling your weekend plans. You have no idea how much this means to me."

"I do, sis. All last week I figured it could take weeks or months to get the kids back to you. Sean really blew it though, coming after you like this. He's going to be in a shitload of trouble with his commanding officer over the abuse and now the DUI. The whole thing will blow open next week. He can't hide any more."

"I'm sorry it came to this, but he caused this mess all by himself. He didn't need any help from me."

"His career is over even without the abuse. Once the civilian courts are finished with him, he'll stand trial before a military court. The fact that he's Special Forces may be the only thing that keeps him in. Even still, he may not get any more deployments."

Andrea sighed. "It's a relief to hear he might not be deployed again. For a lot of reasons." Andrea picked up two pair of small boots and walked towards the house. "C'mon, there's fresh coffee and cookies. Flynn has been a busy man getting ready for the kids."

"He and Gregory are a couple, right?"

"Yes. Any problem with that?"

"Well, no." Richard scuffed his foot at a stone, kicking it away. "It's just that they seem so normal."

"Exactly. They're wonderful people who have been very good to me, even though I was a total stranger until ten days ago."

After paying his fine, Richard left the courtroom with Sean and headed towards the borrowed pickup.

"What's going to happen with your truck?" Richard asked.

"It's been impounded for ninety days. They couldn't take my New Jersey license away because Massachusetts isn't part of some inter-state agreement. So, they impounded my truck instead," Sean said. "Stupid, fucking assholes. I don't need this shit."

Richard shook his head. "What you don't need is another DUI, man. If Massachusetts was part of that inter-state agreement you'd probably be going back to New Jersey in a prison bus."

ANDREA HAD PUT SIMON AND EMILY TO BED and was reading them a story when her phone chirped on the dresser across the room. Both children's eyelids were drooping. The quiet ring barely roused them. Andrea kept reading to them softly and heard the chime that said she had a message.

A few minutes later she closed the book and leaned forward to kiss each of their satiny foreheads. She sat there for a long minute studying their sleeping faces. Finally, she stood up and went over to get her phone. She was in the kitchen when she retrieved the message. Carol and Devin were in the solarium talking quietly. Flynn and Gregory had gone home.

"Ms. Garrett. This is the state troopers' office calling. There's been an accident. You need to call St. Luke's Emergency as soon as possible. Here's the number..."

Carol jumped when she heard the moaning cry and ran to the kitchen, with Devin right behind her. "Andrea, what's wrong?"

Andrea was staring at her phone and looked up at them, her face raw with emotion. "There's been an accident. I have to get to St. Luke's right away. Both Richard and Sean are in critical condition."

"THIS IS SURREAL. WHAT COULD HAVE HAPPENED?" Andrea paced back and forth in the brightly-lit waiting area. "Richard's a good driver."

"Could have been a deer." Carol saw the young resident who had treated Andrea walking towards them. His face revealed nothing.

"Ms. Garrett. Sorry to meet you again under these circumstances." He held two clipboards in his hand. "Your husband and brother are both in surgery. The police say they hit a moose, their truck rolled and then hit a tree."

"How bad is it?" Andrea was joined by Carol, who put an arm around her.

The resident looked at the top clipboard. "Your brother has a broken shoulder and cracked pelvis. There's internal bleeding and a ruptured spleen. His spleen is being removed. He'll be staying with us until he's stable enough to be transferred to a military hospital."

Looking at the second clipboard, he said, "Your husband has a compound fracture to the right arm and undetermined head injuries. Both are bruised from the airbags deploying and—"

"What do you mean undetermined head injuries?" Andrea pressed a palm against her forehead.

"The MRI shows bruising in the brain. We won't know for a few days whether there's been brain damage and what the nature of that damage might be. He'll probably require a lot of rehabilitation."

Andrea put a hand out and steadied herself against the wall.

"Your husband is on active status in the military?" The resident queried.

"Yes, why?"

"We'll be asked to stabilize him so he can be transferred. I hear Womack Medical Center at Fort Bragg has a good traumatic brain injury rehab program. There's also Walter Reed."

Andrea stared at the resident and then looked up at Carol as tears welled up and flowed freely. "Oh my God, Carol. I don't know if I can handle all this."

Carol hugged her tightly. "You can and will handle it. You'll have all the help you need, I promise."

Andrea let herself be led to a chair. She barely registered Carol handing her a cup of steaming coffee from a vending machine. *My brother and my husband both in surgery. Sean with head injuries.* She went numb as they waited for more news.

"YOUR BROTHER IS OUT OF SURGERY, MS. GARRETT." The resident's eyes were bleary from lack of sleep. "He's in recovery. You should be able to see him within the next half hour if all goes well."

"What about my husband?" Andrea barely registered the presence of other people in the room or the images on the wall-mounted television.

"I don't have any word, yet. I'll let you know as soon as I do."

Andrea paced back and forth and then stopped in front of Carol. "I can't ask you to stay here all night. Please, go home. I'll rent a car and find my way back once I know how they're doing. I can sleep on a couch."

"I'm not leaving you, Andrea." Carol patted the spot beside her. "Come and sit down. I told you, you won't be going through this alone."

"I don't know what I'm going to do, Carol. I'm supposed to start with Val the day after tomorrow." Andrea put her head in her hands. "My ex is in critical condition. My brother isn't much better. My children are with Flynn at your farm. I haven't moved into my apartment. Ask me if I'm feeling overwhelmed."

"You need to break everything down into separate components. Otherwise, it will overwhelm you, trust me." Carol put an arm around Andrea and gathered her in close. "You need to work through this one step at a time."

"But I don't even know what the first step needs to be!" Andrea looked up. Tears streamed down her face. "I can't take Sean back, and I can't care for him. After what he's done to me…" She put her head in her hands and sobbed. "I can't take on his care. I just can't. My children need me."

Carol rubbed her back. "No one will ever blame you for putting your children first. Sean will have the support of the military during his rehabilitation. Making the children your first priority will help you see the path for all the rest.

"You have to believe that, whatever happens, it will be for the best, Andrea. You can't pin your future and the future of your children on what happens to Sean now."

Andrea shook her head, as if trying to clear it. "This is not the time to try to make any plans, I know. Right now, my mind is swirling. I just can't get any perspective."

They both looked up as the resident walked into the waiting area with someone whose cap suggested he was part of a surgical team.

"Ms. Garrett? I'm Doctor Somerset. I led the surgical team for your husband's surgery. There's been a complication."

Carol put her arm around Andrea as they both waited for the surgeon's next words.

"Your husband had a seizure during the surgery to relieve pressure in his brain. We have no idea what further damage it caused. But it's clear that he suffered a level of brain trauma that guarantees long-term damage. On top of which I found evidence of a previous brain injury. Was your husband ever hit by a car or subjected to a blast of some kind? Does he play contact sports?"

Andrea's eyes went wide. "Three years ago, on his second deployment, his unit was escorting a resupply convoy when they were ambushed. He told me he couldn't hear for a week. There were multiple explosions. He also had several head injuries playing football and hockey."

The surgeon shook his head. "We're just starting to learn about traumatic brain injuries. I don't know much about them myself yet. But I do know every blow to the head causes some damage. The more blows, the worse it gets. Your husband could be in for a very long haul in rehabilitation."

Andrea turned into Carol's arms and sobbed. "I can't deal with this. I just can't."

"WE SAW HER BROTHER BEFORE WE LEFT. They took out his spleen. He'll be stabilized for a couple of weeks and then moved somewhere closer to his home base." Carol changed into an emerald green silk dressing gown embroidered with dragons. "Andrea is devastated. She can't bring herself to take on Sean again. She needs to focus on the children, but she's worried about managing Sean's affairs. She has power of attorney over him and his health care decisions."

"Is she going ahead with moving into the apartment and working for Val?" Devin asked.

"She is. She's very clearly focused on the children. Told me Sean's parents will have to come forward and take over with him."

"She's a gutsy young woman, I'll give you that. By the way, the kids are wonderful. Flynn and I had a ball with them today." He walked over and wrapped his arms around her. "I have to say, being an honorary grandpa feels pretty good. And you're one sexy grandma, lady." He nuzzled her neck noisily.

"I don't feel especially sexy at the moment, my dear. I am severely sleep deprived." Carol leaned back into his embrace.

"Okay. You're right. But you can't blame me for feeling a little randy. You look edible."

"Hmm. Speaking of edible. I'm hungry. Anything to eat in this place?"

"I think I could rustle you up something."

CHAPTER SEVEN

VAL DROVE UP THE LANE SHARP AT EIGHT O'CLOCK ON MONDAY MORNING. Andrea was waiting for her, with her new steel-toed boots, a ball cap, a lunch bag, and a grim look on her face.

"Heard about the accident. You sure you want to work today?" Val spoke out the window as Andrea walked towards her.

"I can't not work, Val." Opening the passenger door she looked on the seat in surprise. "What're these?"

"They're the keys to our old van. We'll go get it after we check the latest lambs at the Sheridan farm next door. Then you can head off to the hospital this afternoon after our last appointment."

"Oh, Val. Thanks so much. I didn't want to ask Carol. She spent half the night with me at the hospital and part of yesterday, too. Today is her only day off this week."

"Let's get going. We have a whole passel of lambs to check over. Looks like it'll rain later. You got any rain gear?"

"I'll be fine. We'll be in a barn, right?"

"We can pick up a slicker at the shop. The rain should hold off until this afternoon. At least that's what my joints are telling me." She shifted the truck into gear and aimed it down the driveway.

MOMENTS LATER, ANDREA WAS LOOKING UP AT ANOTHER VICTORIAN HOME. Unlike Carol and Devin's, it had a somewhat shabby appearance and windows that didn't look like they'd been cleaned in years.

"Would I be wrong to guess that there's no woman here?"

Val looked up at the house and nodded. "Emma died six years ago. We were close friends for many years. Tom and Kyle don't seem to know much about housekeeping. Strange though, they keep the barn neat and tidy."

"Sounds like Emma took care of the rest."

"Let's go see the lambs." Val climbed out of the truck favoring her left knee. "Some are just a day old."

"Wonder why no one's come out to see us," Andrea said. "They must know we're here."

"Let's just say Thomas and Kyle Sheridan aren't conversationalists these days. Kyle used to be like his mother. She was outgoing and loved to laugh."

As they stepped into the cool darkness of the cavernous barn, pigeons flapped away noisily. Andrea looked around with curiosity. She hadn't been in a barn, other than Devin's horse stable, in years. She breathed in the smell of hay, corn feed, and the distinct smell of damp wool. *This is where I belong. In a barn, with animals. It's all I ever wanted or needed.* She smiled.

She was startled from her musings by the appearance of a tall, lanky man who came towards her drying his hands on a frayed towel. An ancient straw fedora was perched on a tangle of blonde curls that almost reached his broad shoulders. He was followed by a wary black and white border collie.

"Hi. Kyle Sheridan. The lambing jugs are out back."

Andrea looked up into soft blue eyes framed by amazingly long eyelashes. She blinked a couple of times, felt a blush rising up her throat and quickly stuck out her hand. "I'm Andrea Garrett. I'll be working with Val to check over the lambs."

"I know. The lambing jugs are back there." He ignored her outstretched hand. "Just mucked out some pens. Don't think my hands are very clean."

Andrea swallowed and drew herself up as tall as she could and put a small smile on her face. "I'll just go back and get started then. Good to meet you, Kyle." The dog watched her but stayed close to his master's side.

"HOW MANY LAMBS YOU FIGURE WE'LL LOSE THIS YEAR?" Thomas Sheridan, an older version of his son, had watched them in silence for several minutes.

Val and Andrea stood up and stretched. Val massaged her

lower back. They were each in a separate pen, as the ewes and their newborns bonded and learned to nurse.

"You know you'll lose a few, always do." Val leaned down to check the abdomen of one of the lambs. It felt taut; the sign of successful nursing. "So far, all but a few are nursing well. Andrea managed to get a couple of the weaker ones going already. Think we'll take a break for lunch now. Come back at it in half an hour to finish checking the rest."

Val stretched somewhat stiffly. "Mind if we clean up and use your facilities, Tom?"

"You can use the bathroom next to the mud room. You know where it is. Mind you take off your boots before you go in the kitchen."

"Thomas Sheridan, I know to take my boots off. Been coming to this farm since Kyle was a baby. Every year, you say the same thing." Val smiled over at Andrea. "C'mon Andrea. His bark is worse than his bite. I'm hungry."

Andrea stepped into the old kitchen and looked around in dismay. Everything was tidy but without color or charm to relieve its stark lines. A heavy round pedestal table dominated the middle of the room. A dusty sideboard held piles of papers and bills, while a shiny coffee maker appeared to be the only convenience.

Kyle and his father came into the kitchen, making it seem smaller by their presence.

"I sure could use a cup of fresh coffee, Tom, if you're offering." Val winked at Andrea and sat down at the table with her lunch bag in front of her. As she removed its contents, she smirked. Tom shuffled over to the machine to organize a pot.

"You got a girlfriend yet, Kyle?" Val took out half a sandwich and took a large bite.

Andrea watched Kyle blush crimson at the question and put her head down. A very small smile played at the edges of her mouth as she forked up some salad she'd brought.

"No time for women, especially during lambing." Kyle walked past them and opened the fridge door.

Andrea saw its meager contents and was sure she smelled something that belonged in the compost bin she'd seen out back.

He sat down with a hunk of bread and a plastic container of barbeque chicken. He didn't bother with a plate. A glass of water was his only libation.

"Gregory says Andrea is a horse whisperer. Seems you two might have something to talk about." Val munched on her sandwich.

Kyle crooked one eyebrow. He glanced at Andrea but turned back to his eating. He ate methodically, chewing slowly and washing each mouthful down with some water.

"A horse whisperer. Where'd you learn that?"

"It's not something I learned. I didn't even know until Gregory said it." Andrea gazed out the large window over the kitchen sink. A fat sparrow flitted about outside looking for flies. "I hear you're one, too."

"So I'm told." He took another bite of bread. "Around here, the animals are about the only thing to talk to." He looked at his father, who was eating a peanut butter and jam sandwich.

Val broke the silence. "There's a few lambs still having trouble nursing. Andrea, do you mind stopping by after your hospital visit to check in on them? We can work with them awhile before we leave this afternoon. I'll be looking in on Martin Kehoe's lambs tonight. We're going to be hopping for at least another week."

Andrea nodded. "I'll drop by about eight o'clock."

Val looked at the two men and cleared her throat. "Thanks for the sterling conversation, gentlemen. Just so you know, your new neighbor here has her only brother and her ex-husband both recovering from surgery at St. Luke's." She pushed her chair back noisily.

"What happened?"

Andrea looked at Kyle. "They hit a moose. The truck rolled and smashed into a tree."

"Moose are pretty scarce." Kyle tore off a piece of chicken and stuck it in his mouth. "Aren't more than a thousand in all of Massachusetts."

"Well, there's only nine hundred and ninety-nine of them left now." Andrea finished her apple juice and put everything back in her lunch bag. She stood up with Val. "See you later."

"ARE THEY ALWAYS SO TALKATIVE?" Andrea massaged the teats of a large ewe, who was leaning heavily against her. The lamb was winding around between their legs as she worked.

"When Em got sick and then died in just four months, Kyle seemed to curl into himself. Didn't help that his father was in denial that there was anything wrong. He told people she just had a bad flu."

Andrea guided the tiny lamb to his mother and helped him find the teat. She stood up with satisfaction when the little fellow latched on so firmly the ewe put her head down and nudged him, as if to say *take it easy*.

"Almost done here. One more pen to check and we'll go pick up the van." The women continued to work in companionable silence as lambs frisked around them and a soft spring rain began falling.

ANDREA WALKED BRISKLY THROUGH THE RAIN and into the hospital. Making her way to her brother's room, she found him flat on his back staring out the window.

"How's the shoulder?" She smiled brightly and reached out to touch him. Her smile quickly faded when he turned his head towards her.

"What's wrong, little Ricky?" She used the nickname he disliked to try and lighten his mood. He just shook his head.

"I'll be okay, Andy. The pain's pretty intense. I pushed the bell about ten minutes ago."

"I'll be right back." Andrea patted his hand and watched for a smile that wouldn't come.

When she reached the nurses' station, there were three talking to each other. "Excuse me? My brother is in a lot of pain. Could one of you help, please?"

The young nurse looked apologetic. "I'm sorry, but he's not supposed to have more medication for about another half hour."

"Well, he's in pain now. That can't be good for him. I'd appreciate it if you'd page the doctor on duty to come by and see me." Andrea was looking way up at the tall the nurse, but she squared her shoulders and spoke firmly. "Please, come with me. Maybe we can shift him into a more comfortable position."

She waited while the page was put through and then strode down the hall with the nurse in tow.

"I've asked them to page the doctor," Andrea said as she and the nurse helped Richard change positions to take some pressure off his pelvis. She watched him grimace in pain and saw his face turn ashen.

"Richard, how is the pain on a scale of one to ten?" Andrea knew her twin was in intense pain or he wouldn't have said anything and just toughed it out.

"It's fifteen. Dammit. It's excruciating."

"I'll put an urgent page out to Dr. Kelly and to get the charge nurse here with something to ease this. I'm so sorry, I had no idea you were in this much pain." The nurse scurried out of the room.

"Thank God you were here, Andy." Richard spoke through clenched teeth. His eyes were closed. "If I lie perfectly still, it's not quite as bad."

"Yeah, right. And I'm six feet tall." Andrea tried to keep the worry out of her voice.

"Any word on Sean?"

"I'm going to see him after I know you're comfortable and out of pain. He's being kept in a drug-induced coma to reduce the chance of another seizure. It could be a week or two before they bring him out." Andrea gave silent thanks. "It's the reprieve I need to get my life in order before I have to deal with him or his parents."

"Are they coming east?"

"No. I told them there was no point. He's unconscious. I'm close by. They don't know about the divorce yet, and now's not the time to tell them," Andrea said.

The charge nurse and doctor arrived together. After checking his vitals and speaking with his patient, the doctor authorized an increased dose of morphine and then left.

Andrea watched as the medicine began to take effect and breathed a sigh of relief. Richard's hands were no longer clenched into tight fists and the monitor showed his blood pressure was coming down.

"I'm going to leave you now and check in on Sean. Then I have to get back to the farm next to Devin's to see some lambs that are having nursing issues. I'll be back tomorrow after work. Enjoy the drugs!"

He was already snoring softly as she left the room. Andrea smiled as she walked towards the elevator. *I haven't lost my touch when it comes to herding people to get something done*, she thought.

ANDREA STIFLED A YAWN AS SHE PULLED UP TO THE SHERIDAN BARN. She could see lights on inside as she changed from her shoes back into her work boots. *With luck*, she thought, *I can be out of here in half an hour and be back in time to tuck Emily into bed for the night.*

All was quiet in the barn apart from small rustling sounds. The ewes and their lambs were settling in for the night. As she neared the lambing jug where they had isolated the lambs with nursing or health issues, she saw Kyle's hat hung on a hook. Below it, the border collie looked up at her, its eyes alert and golden in the soft light.

"Well. Who are you?" She squatted in front of the compact dog and slowly held her hand out for sniffing inspection. "I guess you'd be the boss of all the ewes and lambs in here, right?"

The dog kept looking at her but didn't move. Its tail lay still.

"Well, I'd best get to work. Time for social chitchat another time, perhaps." Andrea stood and stepped forward into a pool of soft light. Kyle was squatting down to examine the umbilical area of one of the lambs.

He spoke without looking up. "That's Rosie. She's a working dog. Once she works with you and the sheep she'll be more communicative.

"I haven't seen one before," he said, "but I think this little ewe lamb has an umbilical hernia. You know anything about them?"

"Nothing specific. I can call Val though and check with her."

"Yes, please."

Andrea went to the van and retrieved her iPhone. Walking

back to the barn, she called Val and explained the situation. She put the phone on video and handed it to Kyle.

"It's on video. Just put it in close to where the cord is and scan slowly so Val can see."

Kyle looked a bit confused but did as he was told. After a few seconds, he handed the phone back to Andrea.

"Okay, Val says it is a very small umbilical hernia. I can cleanse everything with iodine, stitch it up and she should be fine. Good thing you saw it, Kyle. Do you have a needle and thread handy?"

"My mother's sewing kit is in the sideboard in the kitchen. I have iodine here. I'll stay with the lamb. I don't know what needle you want." Kyle stopped talking and Andrea smiled, wondering if he'd spoken that many words in as many days.

"So, your phone sent live video to Val. Isn't that something? I don't even have a mobile." Kyle had picked up the lamb and was cradling it in his arms.

"It's called telemedicine. It's been around for years but, with the smart phones now, it's so easy. I'll be back shortly." Andrea thought about how gentle he was with the newborn lamb.

She sprinted over to the house and carefully removed her boots in the mud room before knocking on the kitchen door. She smiled ruefully as Tom opened the door and she stepped onto the floor that probably hadn't been washed in months.

"I need your wife's sewing kit. Kyle says it's in the sideboard. One of the lambs has an umbilical hernia."

Tom stepped aside without a word. Andrea realized there were no cooking smells. *It's so sad*, she thought, *Emma must have been such a force in their lives. They're both lost without her.*

As she pulled out the antique sewing box and looked inside, she almost dropped it. It was littered with mouse droppings. She carefully lifted out a plastic-covered pack of needles that appeared untouched. The thread was a different story. *Thank goodness for iodine*, she thought.

"You'll want to clean this out, Mr. Sheridan. You've had rodent visitors." She put the box on the kitchen counter next to where she hoped there was a garbage pail and quickly escaped.

Back in the barn, moments later, she washed her hands thoroughly before dousing the entire spool of thread and needle package in iodine.

"I left the sewing basket with your father to clean out. It's full of mouse droppings." She was busy with her antiseptic preparations and didn't see a small smile play over Kyle's face or a little sparkle come into his eyes.

"My father won't truck with cleaning out a woman's sewing basket. For him, that would be crossing into foreign territory."

Andrea looked up and caught the smile as he chuckled. She smiled back.

"What do you think he'll do?"

"Where'd you put the basket?"

"On the counter, next to the sink. Why?" Andrea measured off a length of thread and threaded it through the eye of the needle.

"Well, unless I take care of it, it will still be there in a month."

"Then you'd best take care of it, Kyle Sheridan. And get some mouse traps, too. From what I saw, there's a good chance you have a colony in the house."

"Probably do. You like telling people what to do?"

"Only if I have to." Andrea soaked a piece of gauze in iodine as Kyle cradled the lamb on its back. "Hold her firm. It won't take more than a minute but she'll struggle. I've sutured before many times with my dad instructing me, just not a lamb this small."

Andrea spread back the lamb's soft wool from the small opening. After cleansing the area thoroughly, she pinched together the skin flaps and put in three quick stitches.

"There. Done. You can let her go now."

Kyle released the lamb as the ewe stayed close by. The lamb went over to nurse as if nothing had happened. "Nice work."

"I'll look in tomorrow morning before I go to work and check my stitches. I'm pretty sure they'll hold. You know how to reach me if anything else comes up." Andrea's stomach growled so loudly they both heard it.

"Excuse me!" Andrea laughed. "I haven't had dinner yet and haven't eaten anything since lunch. I'm starved."

"Sorry. I've kept you from your dinner." Kyle's voice was quiet.

"And my children. I have two. We're all staying with Carol and Devin for a couple more days."

"Val says it's your ex-husband who is at St. Luke's. How is he?"

"Not good. He'll probably never regain full mental capacity. The surgeon told me he has traumatic brain injuries. I don't know what those are, but I intend to find out."

"I heard on NPR that a lot of servicemen are coming back with them. They call it TBI, for short. It didn't have a name until Iraq and Afghanistan. But I'm sure it's been around as long as there've been bombs. They called it shell shock back in World War Two."

"You've heard of it?" Andrea's hunger was quickly forgotten. "Even the surgeon wasn't really sure what to tell me."

"Basically, any injury to the brain causes some level of trauma. For our guys overseas, it's caused mostly by bomb blasts and vehicle accidents. With a bomb, there's a wall of air pressure created when it goes off. The nearby soldiers get thrown to the ground or against an object. The brain slams against the back of the skull, rebounds and slams against the front of the skull."

Andrea was intrigued. "So why are they so dangerous?"

"The brain is soft, like jello. The skull is hard as a coconut shell. I guess it's like putting jello in a bowl until it's almost full, putting the lid on and then shaking it hard. The jello would get cracks in it and start breaking apart. If that was your brain, you'd be in trouble."

They were now standing beside her van. Rosie was watching from the barn door. Andrea wanted to know more: about traumatic brain injury, but also, she realized, about Kyle Sheridan. *This is not the man I met this morning,* she mused. *There's a mind at work here. A mind I'd like to know more about.*

"Kyle, thank you for telling me about this, but I need to get going. I think I've missed my children's bedtime. Want to have a coffee tomorrow morning? Flynn is taking care of my daughter and son for the day."

"What are your children's names?"

"Emily and Simon."

"Good names. Solid names." Kyle closed the van door as Andrea got in. "I'll warn you, I'm not very good at making coffee."

"I'll show you. I'm not much of a baker or cook, but I can make a fine pot of coffee." Andrea smiled up at him. "I'll come over about half past six. Don't start the coffee until I get here, right?"

"Right. See you then."

As Andrea drove away, she looked into the rearview mirror and smiled. Kyle was still standing where she had left him, a dark silhouette standing by the light above the barn door. Rosie had joined him. *I think we have more to talk about, Kyle Sheridan, much more.*

CHAPTER EIGHT

ANDREA WOKE UP TO SOMETHING TICKLING HER FACE. She crooked one eye open slightly and saw Emily's teddy bear lying beside her, while its owner brushed a blue jay feather against her ear.

She growled. "Who is that tickling my ear?"

A bubbling giggle was accompanied by more tickling.

"Is that my Peanut?" Andrea turned over on her back and opened both eyes. She smiled and reached out for a sleepy hug. "Come here, Peanut. Where'd you get that beautiful feather?"

"Flynn found it. The blue jays eat the paint off his house and leave a feather to pay for it." Emily stroked the bright blue and black feather.

"I've never heard of blue jays eating house paint." Andrea smiled, sure Flynn was making the story up.

"He showed me. There's a big spot with no paint." Emily climbed off the bed. "I'm hungry."

Andrea smiled and turned back the covers. "How about we go down to the kitchen and get breakfast organized for everyone? Looks like you're the first one awake, today."

Together, they went down the stairs.

THE SUN WAS JUST PEAKING OVER THE TREETOPS AS ANDREA SHRUGGED INTO A JACKET. "I'm off to the Sheridan farm to check on the lambs." Andrea planted warm kisses on Emily and Simon's heads as she tucked her lunch bag under her arm. "Thanks for staying with them, Flynn. I'm interviewing a couple of people Val recommended. Hope to have a sitter by Monday."

"No problem. I hope you're putting moves on Kyle, sweetie. He is one gorgeous man." Flynn set a fresh loaf of bread on the counter and went to sit with Emily and Simon. "We're going to make a batch of muffins together, my beauties."

"Have fun!" Andrea looked back as Simon climbed onto Flynn's lap and gave him a hug. *I made the right decision by deciding to move here,* she thought. *This is a good place to raise my children.*

AS ANDREA DROVE UP THE SHERIDAN'S DRIVEWAY she realized, with pleasant surprise, that Kyle and Rosie were standing at the top of the small hill waiting for her. The sun bathed his silhouette in a warm glow. *You're right, Flynn, he is a gorgeous male.*

"Good morning, Kyle." Andrea pulled the van up next to him. "Mornin' Rosie."

"Good morning to you, Andrea." Kyle took off his straw fedora and wiped a hand across his forehead. "Going to be hot today."

"Between the rain and heat, everything will be growing faster than usual." Andrea smiled and stepped out of the van.

Kyle towered over her. "Let's go start Coffee Making 101. We can come back and check the lambs later. Rosie will watch over them and let us know if anything is wrong."

Andrea looked at Rosie, who had heard her name and was waiting for a command.

"Rosie. Go. Lie down." Kyle pointed to the barn.

They watched as the dog quickly trotted to the barn door and lay down to guard its occupants.

"You'll have to meet Bonnie and Clyde, and Taco Bell."

"Who are they?"

"They're my horses. I bought them about the time my mother got sick. A farmer we knew was downsizing his operation. The price was too good to pass up." They walked towards the mud room. "She loved to feed them apples and would sit in a chair and just watch them."

"It's good she had something like that to enjoy in her final days." Andrea looked up at him with a smile. They stepped into the mud room and dutifully took off their boots.

Andrea's eyes widened in surprise when she stepped into the kitchen. "You washed the floor!"

Kyle smiled and dropped his head. "It was really bad. I had to change the water five times before it stopped being gray."

Andrea chuckled. "I couldn't believe it when your father made us take our boots off each time we came in."

"My mother always insisted on it. She even made us take our coveralls off and leave them in the mud room. Said she could smell every animal and bird that had ever been in the barn. Don't think my father wanted Val taking hers off, though. Just the boots." He grinned at her. "Some things best stay covered."

Andrea laughed at the thought of a half-naked Val. "My mother was the same whenever my father or I had been to a farm. I find the smells comforting and natural. They don't bother me at all." Andrea made a beeline for the coffee maker. "Is your tap water good?"

"It's very pure. I tested it several times when I was in university and had access to a lab."

Andrea's eyebrows went up. "What did you study?"

"Sustainable agriculture." Kyle stood beside Andrea as she put water in the carafe.

"How do you prefer your coffee?" She had opened the can and was standing with the scoop in her hand.

"I guess I'd call it medium strong."

"That's the way I like mine, too." Andrea filled the carafe to the six cup line. "So, for medium strong coffee you would put in two scoops for every three cups. For six cups, that's four scoops."

"My father puts in one scoop for each cup and then one for the pot."

"Do you like it?" Andrea turned on the coffee maker, acutely aware of his nearness.

"Not really."

"Val called it sludge."

Kyle laughed. The throaty sound welled up out of nowhere. Andrea laughed back, as the coffee maker started gurgling hot water over the grounds.

"Where is your father?" They both stood close together as they watched the coffee gradually filling the pot.

"I told him we needed fresh hay. He's gone off to pick up a load."

Andrea felt warmth creeping up her neck and hoped she wasn't blushing. "So, you cleared out your father because I was coming over?"

"I did."

"Why?" Andrea watched his color deepen.

He coughed. Andrea almost strained to hear his soft reply. "I didn't want to share you."

"Is that the Sheridan way of saying you wanted to spend some time alone with me?" Andrea smiled and cocked her head to one side. The coffee maker sputtered as the last of the water poured into the filter.

"You're not making this easy." Kyle was red to the roots of his hair.

It was Andrea's turn to blush. "I'm sorry, Kyle. I didn't mean to make you feel uncomfortable."

"I'll get over it," Kyle said. "Let's get our coffee and go check the lambs."

"Now, we have a plan." Andrea breathed a deep sigh of relief. *Take it slow and easy,* she chided herself. *This man has been out of social circulation way too long and definitely hasn't been around a woman for a while.*

"How's the ewe lamb doing? The one I sutured?" Andrea picked up her mug of steaming coffee after handing one to Kyle. Their hands brushed together briefly. For Andrea, the touch was electric.

"Looks fine to me. The stitches are still in, and there's no redness or swelling that I can see."

"Let's go confirm that diagnosis." Andrea led the way to the barn as the sun burst in its full glory over the horizon.

A HALF HOUR LATER, KYLE LED ANDREA THROUGH TO THE BACK OF THE BARN. Stopping by a large sack of apples, he took out three and then opened the door into a large paddock. Rosie stayed close behind them as they stepped into the sunshine.

"Rosie, lie down." The wiry dog dropped like a stone and lay there, without moving, her eyes alert as the horses' ears pricked up.

Andrea heard the horses begin whinnying and moving towards them. She watched in fascination as two ebony black animals shook their heads and ambled across the large enclosure, followed by a smaller chestnut-colored horse.

"Andrea, meet Bonnie and Clyde and behind them is Taco Bell, or Taco for short."

"Oh, Kyle. They're magnificent!"

"Bonnie and Clyde are Canadian horses. I'm not a breeder at this point, but Bonnie is expecting in a few weeks."

"I thought she looked quite rounded out." Andrea smiled and smoothed her hand down the somewhat shorter mare. "You're going to have a beautiful colt, Bonnie."

The mare looked at Andrea and snickered softly. Kyle gave her an apple for the horse.

"Taco is a Morgan horse. That's the official state horse of Massachusetts."

"She's a beauty. I love the color of her coat. How old is she?"

Kyle handed Andrea another apple. "She's three now. She's very gentle. I love riding her."

Andrea reached up to scratch the side of Taco's head with one hand and gave her the apple with the other. "You're so lovely, young lady."

She looked over at Kyle. "Is that it for animals?"

"There's Portia. That's my dad's pot-bellied pig. She's his buddy. He talks to her more than he talks to me." With Rosie again at their heels, Kyle led her back into the coolness of the barn. "She has her own house off to the side over here. My dad built it for her."

They could hear snorting and snuffling as they got closer. "Our property is completely fenced so she has the run of the place. She's created her own trails around the farm."

Andrea giggled as she spied the pig. "It never occurred to me to think of something that big as being cute."

At the sound of their voices, Portia stood and trundled her large body over.

"She's looking for food. She'll do anything for food." Kyle was ready with an apple. "My dad's taught her some tricks. She's quite smart.

"We have a small herd of goats, too. Between them, the sheep, horses and Portia, the pastures get a good workout and so does Rosie."

"You love this, don't you?" Andrea leaned against the rail fence next to Portia's over-sized dog house.

"I really do. My dad and I make a decent living doing something that's good for the earth."

"That's how I feel about my work now. I'm doing what I love without harming anyone or any thing."

Kyle looked at Andrea for a long moment. "Well, Rosie and I'd best be getting back to work."

Andrea sighed. "Me too. Thanks very much for the coffee and the tour, Kyle."

"If anything comes up with the lambs, I'll call you." He took the empty mug from her hand.

"Maybe we could get together again, sometime. I've been riding with Carol and Devin in the morning. Perhaps we could go riding one day."

Kyle walked her out of the barn, setting the mugs on a work bench along the way. "Maybe we could."

ANDREA AND VAL WERE ASSISTING AT THE BREACH BIRTH OF A CALF. The cow had been in labor for several hours before the owner called.

"That was a nice piece of team work on the hernia, Andrea. With the smart phones, you and I don't have to be together. It's amazing how far we've come in just a few years."

"I know." Andrea grinned. "Kyle couldn't get over the way we used the video to let you do the diagnosis and then I did the suturing. He was impressed. We even had coffee together this morning, although I had to show him how to make a good pot."

"Thank you for that. The crap Tom served yesterday was vile. You're lucky you didn't have any. My stomach was upset all afternoon."

"Thought you looked a bit off. Well, I think we'll be safe from now on. They also have mice in the house. Got Kyle convinced he needs to work on that."

"That's a lot of progress in one day, young lady." Val looked over at her with a grin. "You have designs on him?"

Andrea blushed. "No designs yet, but he really is interesting. He knows about traumatic brain injury. Sean has traumatic brain injuries, and I really want to know more."

"About traumatic brain injuries or Kyle?" The cow bellowed as Val reached in up to her elbows to ease the calf around.

"Both. He's really good looking, and I adore his hair. I can't imagine *him* with a military spit and polish buzz cut." Andrea grinned as she and Val watched the calf slide out of the birth canal. "If he's like his dad, he'll never go bald."

Val peeled off the elbow length rubber gloves she'd been wearing as the cow stood up to check her new progeny. "The Sheridans are complicated, but Tom and Kyle are good people. They've just never recovered from Emma's illness and death."

"From what I've seen of Kyle, he's a rescue project I wouldn't mind pursuing."

"Just be prepared for some Sheridan resistance."

"When I set my sights on something, resistance is futile." Andrea grinned at Val as the calf stood up on wobbly legs. Its mother smelled it thoroughly and then started licking it.

"I was hoping you'd say that." Val crossed her arms over her ample bosom. "Those two men are special to me, and they were very, very special to my friend Em. She'd approve of you."

Andrea smiled. "I'd like to think so."

ANDREA STEPPED INTO CAROL'S KITCHEN and followed the sounds of childish voices and adult chuckles to the solarium. She was bone tired and hungry, but she felt exhilarated. She'd helped deliver her first calf since before she went to university. *I didn't forget a thing.* She smiled to herself.

"Where's my Dancing Peanut? And where is my big boy Simon?"

"Mommy! Carol and Devin have a puppy!" Emily stayed sitting on the floor next to a cardboard box that held a small ball of fur.

"Oh, my. He's so little." Andrea walked over and slumped onto a nearby couch. "Where's my hug?"

Emily jumped up and leaned in to hug and kiss her mother but quickly returned to sit beside the box holding the furry treasure.

Carol smiled. "We weren't expecting this little guy for another two weeks, but his mother refused to nurse and the owner called us to take him. He's six weeks old. Chocolate Lab."

"Where's Simon?"

"He's still napping. He hasn't seen the puppy yet. I just got back with him. Can I get you something?" Carol put a hand on Andrea's knee. "You looked bushed."

"Oh, I'll be fine. Just a bit tired and definitely hungry. Helped Val deliver a breech calf this afternoon. I was on a total high. I'm at the crash and burn stage now," she said, "I think I'll take tonight off from going to the hospital. The past week is catching up with me. Up way too late and up far too early."

Carol stood. "Tell you what. I'm off tomorrow and need to do some shopping. Emily and Simon can come with me, and I'll take them over to visit Richard. Is Louise coming down this weekend?"

Andrea laid her head back against a small pillow Carol handed her. "She's coming Saturday. Her sister and parents are going to take care of the kids. Oh, and I have two women lined up to interview to take care of Emily and Simon when I'm working or need some personal time. Val recommended them both, so it's probably just a matter of personal vibes. One is a grandmother."

"Glad Val could help. I don't know everyone around here, yet." Carol rearranged a vase of flowers on a side table and looked out to the paddock. "Devin is on his way in. I'll put out some food we can snack on. I don't think we'll have a formal supper tonight. This is watch the puppy night and come up with his name."

"Can you come and help me in the kitchen, Peanut?" Carol waved to Devin through the window.

"I'll be back, puppy. You sleep." Emily gently patted him. The pup snuggled into the blanket. No one noticed Andrea's eyes close, nor the soft snores as her head drooped to one side.

ANDREA DROVE UP A LONG DRIVEWAY BORDERED BY TALL MAPLES and parked in front of a tidy Victorian house surrounded by cedars and neatly-trimmed shrubs. She wasn't even out of the car when the front door opened and an older woman stepped out, followed by two barking dogs.

"Don't mind them. They're just happy to have company. You must be Andrea. Come in. Come in."

Andrea smiled as the two Jack Russells bounded around her ankles. She stepped forward carefully as the dogs yipped their greetings.

"All right you two. That's enough. Let poor Andrea into the house. Sorry, they have to let off steam for a couple more minutes. Just ignore them."

"Not a problem, Mrs. Henderson. I'm sure you've heard by now that I love all animals."

"I heard you're a horse whisperer. Around here, that puts you at the top of the gossip pole for at least a few more weeks. I've been told to find out as much about you as I can for my book club next week."

Andrea hooted with laughter, her eyes sparkling with mirth. "You're an honest woman, Mrs. Henderson. I like that."

"And you are someone with a good sense of humor. I like that. Please come in. Which do you prefer, coffee or tea?"

"Whatever you're having is fine with me. I like both." Andrea stepped into the front hall and felt like she'd stepped back in time. "Oh, my. Look at that grandfather clock. How old is it? It's beautiful."

Janet Henderson beamed with pride. "My great-great grandfather had that shipped from England. I'd say it's at least two hundred years old. It's in perfect working condition, too. There's a fellow in town who comes by every year to check it."

Andrea gazed around in awe. "I wanted to visit the home of each prospective babysitter or nanny to see how you live. I never expected to see this kind of grandeur. Why do you want the job of looking after my children, Mrs. Henderson?"

"Call me Janet, please. Let's go to the kitchen." She led the way towards the back of the house, past curved hall tables and dainty chairs. "I live alone in this house since my husband passed on. Our three children all live out of state. I have five grandchildren but I only see them once or twice a year. When I heard you were looking for help, I knew I wanted to be around little ones again."

They walked into a large sunny kitchen with gleaming appliances and pine cabinets. "Here we are. Please have a seat, Andrea. How about some Earl Grey?"

"That would be lovely."

"And a muffin?"

"Yes, please." Andrea looked around the spacious, bright kitchen, astounded by the stark contrast between the Sheridan place and this vibrant space full of color and light.

"This kitchen is just wonderful, Janet. Do you do much baking?"

"I'll let you in on one of the poorest kept secrets in the area. I supply the Sweet Repose with quite a few items from that oven over there." She pointed at an ancient oven with six burners and a large cook top. "Back in the day, when we had a lot of workers helping in the fields, I was cooking for twelve at each meal. I made pies six at a time. I could cook two dozen eggs on the griddle."

Andrea looked around in awe. "I can see it, Janet. I think I can even smell it, too. And now you're here, all by yourself."

Janet looked at her. Andrea saw a faint flicker of sadness in her eyes. "Yes, dear, I'm here alone, but this house is so full of happy memories that I don't feel the least bit lonely. Do you know what I mean?"

"I think I do, yes. I used to feel that way after my parents came to visit me when I was at university. When they left on Sunday afternoon, I'd be all by myself again, but I didn't feel lonely. I could still smell my dad's aftershave in the bathroom and my mother's perfume in the closet where she'd hung her clothes."

"Then, you know what I mean. Even though all physical remnants of my husband and children are gone from this house, I have so many other happy associations. When I bake, I can always remember that my husband Peter loved my cranberry orange muffins or that my daughter Shirley still lives for my tart apple pies when she and the family visit. I can never be lonely with those memories warming my heart."

Andrea made her decision. "Janet, if you want the job, it's yours. I'll interview the other lady as back-up for evenings or weekends if I get called in to work. What do you charge?"

"Well, let's make a deal. I know you'd like me to come to your apartment to take care of the children. But, would you be willing to let them come here most days? Then, I could cook and bake at the same time.

"I was thinking of charging you a hundred dollars a week, including their meals when they're here." Janet looked at her expectantly.

Andrea looked at her in surprise. "That is beyond reasonable for two children. We could definitely work this out. I know Emily and Simon would love this place. You sure you want a couple of little ones running around here?"

"They always used to. This house could use a little injection of youth, don't you think?" Janet smiled warmly. "The dogs will be happy, I'm sure."

"When can you start?" Andrea sipped at the fragrant tea.

"You say when, and I'll be there." Janet said, and set a plate of muffins on the table between them.

"How about Monday? I'll move with them into the apartment over the weekend and arrange with Val to start later on Monday so you can all be properly introduced." Andrea flashed a sparkling smile at Janet. "And if you happened to bring a couple of muffins, it would more than likely seal the introduction. My kids are mad about muffins."

"Done. How about I throw in the macaroni and cheese my grandkids love for their lunch?"

"Now you're cooking. They'll love it. Sorry I won't be there to join you!"

"Put a container out and you can bring some to warm up for your lunch. I know Val. She gets kitchen privileges wherever she goes."

CHAPTER NINE

ANDREA LET HERSELF INTO HER NEW APARTMENT and set down the bags she was carrying. *It's starting to take shape,* she thought. *I'm so glad Carol talked me into taking my time to get everything organized for Emily and Simon.*

She looked at her watch. *I'll take two hours to organize and put things away and then go over and see Richard and Sean.* She rotated her head slowly to try and relax her neck muscles. *Thank goodness I have Janet Henderson coming on board. Between her and Carol, I will have a good network as things start to move with Richard and Sean.*

She set to work putting clothes away, hanging things in the closets and getting the beds made. *I have to deal with Sean's situation,* she thought, and felt her neck stiffen all over again. *I can't live with him. I can't care for him, that's for sure. And, I won't put him ahead of Emily and Simon.* She shook her head. *This accident has complicated everything.*

A thought came into her mind that she couldn't push away. *If only he had just died. Everything would be so much easier. But, if he died, I might have lost Richard too. I couldn't bear that.*

She held a sweater of Emily's in her hands and thought of Sean, lying in the hospital bed hooked up to a bank of machines. Putting her face against the sweater, she thought about the inevitable confrontation with her mother-in-law in the coming days. *This won't be pretty,* she mused as she tucked the small sweater into a drawer.

When everything was unpacked and put away, she slowly looked around her daughter's new bedroom. *It needs some pictures,* she thought, *and a couple of lamps. We should go to some spring garage sales.* The thought made her smile. Emily was her little shopper already. She loved trolling garage sales. *It's a way to meet and get to know people, too,* she thought. Andrea smiled and hoped for decent weather over the weekend.

NOTHING HAD CHANGED WHEN ANDREA WENT INTO SEAN'S ROOM. The monitors were quietly showing normal readouts for blood pressure and pulse. The crook of the elbow on the arm that was not in a cast was bruised from IV catheters. The backs of both hands were similarly bruised. Her once-tough husband lay unconscious on the bed, his suntanned face turning pale and sunken. The bruises from the airbag were starting to yellow. It had been almost a week since the accident.

Andrea stood at the foot of the narrow bed and stared at him. She shook her head. Looking at his comatose body, she felt relief wash over her. *Emily and Simon will probably never know him. He was an angry stranger after his last deployment,* she thought. *Emily was afraid of him. Simon is too young to remember him.*

She stared at Sean another long moment, without blinking. *I wish you no harm, Sean. Despite everything, I wish you no harm.* Then she turned on her heels and left the room. Her eyes were dry.

"I THINK THEY'RE DOWN FOR THE NIGHT." Andrea joined Carol and Devin in the solarium and accepted Devin's offer of a glass of wine. "I'm ready to move us all into the apartment. Janet Henderson is going to meet us there first thing Monday morning. We'll move on Saturday and visit garage sales along the way to shop for a few things."

"You realize they may not want to move now, with the puppy being here?" Carol grinned sheepishly and looked at the box near the fireplace. "He wasn't supposed to be here for another two weeks, I swear."

"I hope to get a pet for us, too." Andrea smiled at her. "Sean would never hear of it, which was probably a good thing. He wouldn't have the patience for a pup. I'm sure of it." The thought of Sean turning his temper on a puppy sent a chill down Andrea's spine.

"Besides, Janet has two really cute little Jack Russell terriers," she said. "I'm sure Emily and Simon will be thrilled. And, they can visit the puppy."

"I expect you to be regular weekend dinner guests," Carol said. "As honorary grandparents, we will expect your visits. I also plan to drop by with Gordie once he's trained."

"Gordie. What a cute name. It suits him." Andrea grinned as the puppy poked up his head. "I think he already knows it, too."

"What's the word on Sean?" Devin looked up from the book he was reading.

"They're going to reduce the meds over the next twenty-four hours. Bring him back gradually and monitor him for any sign of a seizure. I've been in touch with his parents and they're on the way." Andrea took a long sip of wine. "I told his mother I've left him and made it very clear I don't have any room for them to stay with me."

Carol sat forward. "How did she react?"

"To put it mildly, she had a complete hissy fit. Told me I'm a lazy leech who doesn't deserve to clean his boots."

"Do you care what she thinks?" Carol looked at her.

"Of course not." Andrea crooked her eyebrows. "I have two beautiful children. As far as I'm concerned, Sean was the sperm donor. He was never a parent in any real sense of the word. He was definitely not a husband any woman would want."

"Sounds like you've made your final decision."

"I have. No matter what happens to Sean, he is no longer part of my life. Except for the paperwork, my marriage is over and has been for a long time. I'm hoping he'll never be part of Emily and Simon's life either."

Carol stood up, walked over, and put her hands on Andrea's arms. "If you were my daughter, I would tell you I'm a hundred and fifty percent supportive of your decision. And I will be behind you to support it, every step of the way."

Andrea's eyes filled with tears. "You may not be my mother, but you make me feel mothered in a very special way. In an adult way. At the very least, you're one of my best friends."

"Count on it, Andrea. And Devin, Flynn, Gregory and Val, too. You have a whole new cheering squad."

"Where are the tissues?" Andrea sniffled with happiness as her phone chirped. "Hello?"

A smile spread over her face. "Hi, Kyle. How's everything?"

She looked at Carol, who dangled a box of tissues in front of her. She smiled a teary no thanks. "What a great idea! Thanks, yes, I know they'd love to see the lambs. We'll be over after breakfast."

By the time the call ended she was beaming. "Seems Kyle wants to meet Emily and Simon."

"And see you again, no doubt." Carol winked at Andrea. "You should bring some of those muffins Janet Henderson gave you to sweeten the deal. Those men don't get anything homemade from what you told me."

"That's a great idea." Andrea grinned. "He's going to make coffee for us. I taught him how to make really good coffee."

THEY PULLED UP AT THE SHERIDAN HOUSE SHORTLY AFTER EIGHT the next morning. Andrea was confident that both children would be fine for several hours. They'd had breakfast. Simon had a fresh diaper. Emily had brought her teddy bear.

"Kyle, hi!" Andrea stepped out of the van. Again, he'd been waiting at the top of the driveway as they drove up. "Where's Rosie?"

"In the barn, watching the ewes that are still in the pens. The rest are out to pasture again."

Kyle walked over and peered into the van. "Hi, Emily. Hi, Simon. Want to see my lambs?"

Andrea was surprised to see Emily reach out her arms to Kyle to be lifted out of her car seat. "This is Kyle, Emily. Say hi?"

"Hi, Kyle. I want to see the lambs." She ignored her teddy bear.

"We call her, Peanut." Andrea said.

"Hi, Peanut. Let's go see my lambs. They're only two days old."

Andrea was left to get Simon out of his seat and follow Kyle and Emily into the dark coolness of the barn.

"The ewes and lambs are all doing really well." Kyle spoke over his shoulder as he led them to the pens. "The ewe lamb with the hernia looks to be healing just fine. Thanks."

Emily and Simon went into a pen together and were immediately surrounded. Andrea and Kyle kept close watch as the children petted animals that were smaller than they were. They chuckled when one lamb butted Simon's behind and sent him sprawling in the clean hay. Rosie looked on from a spot over by a wall.

"They're beautiful children, Andrea." Kyle looked down at her. "They're both being very gentle with the lambs."

"Luckily, they get that from me." Andrea looked on as Emily tried to hug a squirming lamb. She was about to say more when Kyle spoke up.

"How is your husband doing?"

"They're bringing him back to consciousness now. My in-laws are about to descend. The next few days will be interesting, to say the least. I've told them that I'm filing for divorce. My mother-in-law accused me of deserting her son because he is disabled."

"Is that what you're doing?" They both smiled as Simon was again bowled over by a lamb.

"Wonder if there's a diaper change needed here." Andrea didn't want the moment to end. "No, I'm not deserting him. He's had a strong violent streak for a long time. I found out the hard way on our honeymoon. I should have left him before Simon was conceived, but, I was naïve and very lonely after the death of my parents. We should never have married."

"What happened to your parents?"

"They were killed by a teenage drunk."

"And you just have the one brother?"

"He's my twin. We're very close, but Sean is his best buddy. It has really hurt him to see Sean as an abuser." Andrea scooped Simon up in her arms just as he decided the lambs weren't fun anymore.

"How about we go up to the house and change you, buddy? We can all have a muffin." Andrea picked pieces of hay out of Simon's brown curls.

"You brought muffins?" Kyle asked the little girl as he took her by the hand and carefully closed the pen's gate. "Did you make them yourself?"

Emily looked up at Kyle. "No, my babysitter made them. I don't know her, yet."

"You know Janet Henderson?" Andrea set Simon down as they reached the door to the mud room.

"Yes, she's a fine lady and was a very close friend of the family." Kyle helped Emily take off her boots. "She and my mom used to make jam and do canning together. They took turns between their kitchens. Our house smelled so good on those days."

"She and I hit it off right away. Especially when she told me she needed to get lots of information about me so she could gossip with her book club ladies." Andrea smiled as she led Simon towards the bathroom. "We'll be right back."

"DO YOU NEED HELP WITH THE MOVE?" Kyle looked at Andrea and the children sitting at his kitchen table as sunlight streamed through the windows he had finally cleaned. "I have a pickup."

Andrea smiled at him. "Everything will fit in my van, but I could use a couple of strong arms. Hope you don't mind stopping by some garage sales. I need a couple of lamps for Emily's room."

Kyle was lost in that smile. "How about we take everything to your apartment and then see about the garage sales?"

"That would make a lot of sense, although the best stuff will be gone before noon."

"Maybe we could take everything today and leave tomorrow free." Kyle couldn't stop his mouth, even as his mind warned him he probably had no chance with Andrea. *Why would she be interested in a humorless farmer who lives with his surly father? I want to spend more time around this woman. But, I have work to do.* He waited anxiously for her reply.

Andrea beamed a bright smile. "You wouldn't mind? It would be wonderful to take my time and not try to cram everything into one day. I do have the rest of the day off. Val had to go to Boston."

"Mommy, I have to go." Emily tugged Andrea's sleeve.

"Sure, Peanut. There's a little bathroom right next to the mud room. Off you go and remember to flush."

Simon played on the floor with a couple of toy trucks he'd brought along. Kyle looked at him. "Do you think he remembers his father?"

"If I show him a picture, he can identify him, but he never asks for him. He wasn't even a year old when Sean deployed." Andrea took the dishes and cups to the sink to wash them.

"It was really brave of you to break with Sean and start out on your own with two pre-schoolers." Kyle found a tea towel and started drying the dishes beside her. "You're a brave woman, Andrea."

Andrea laughed. "You wouldn't have said that if you'd seen me the night I drove into the ditch. I was terrified by what I was doing. I really bought into the whole for better or for worse concept."

"Until when?" Kyle asked, quietly.

"Until I realized my husband would probably kill me. I want to be here to raise my children and see them grow up." Andrea took the towel from his hands and dried her own.

Kyle saw her tears and reached out to wipe one away. "Let's get you moved into your new apartment."

AS THE LAST BOX WAS BROUGHT IN FROM KYLE'S PICKUP, ANDREA LOOKED AROUND. "That's it. We're done! Who wants to order pizza?" Andrea was met with cheers from Emily and Simon. "You're invited too, Kyle. We'll just get a bigger one. My way to say thanks for all your help."

"That sounds great," he said.

"Why don't you sit down and relax? I'll call in the order, and we'll christen my new plates and cutlery. Would you like a beer or some wine?" Andrea's hand froze on the refrigerator door. *Oh God,* she thought. *I don't really know him. Maybe I shouldn't offer.*

"I'll have one when the pizza gets here. I'll just have some water for now, thanks." Kyle went and sat back in an old-fashioned recliner. "Where did you get this? It's all broken in and comfortable."

"It came with the apartment. Almost all the furniture did. Richard brought the kids' beds and dressers. There is very little we need now. Everyone has been incredibly generous."

They chatted as the children played with toys they hadn't seen for several days.

"How is Richard? I'd like to meet your twin." Kyle grinned. "Just hope he doesn't look like you."

"What do you mean by that?" Andrea looked puzzled.

"Well, you're pretty and petite. Not many guys want to be described that way."

"Ah, well Richard, no, he would not want to be called pretty." Andrea chuckled. "Or petite. And while we're on the topic, what's in the drinking water around here, anyway? Almost every man I've met is six feet tall or more. I only feel normal height when I'm around the children."

They were interrupted by the doorbell. Emily jumped up.

"Emily, don't open the door until we know who it is, remember?"

"But, Mommy, I can *smell* the pizza."

"All right, then. You can open the door."

As Emily opened the door, a large pizza box suddenly formed a cardboard canopy over her head.

"I believe this is for you, young lady." A smiling young woman close to Andrea's age held the box out. "Hi, I'm Joy. Joy O'Connor. Decided to bring it over myself so I could meet you. My aunt, Janet Henderson, told me she's going to be taking care of Emily and Simon."

"Nice to meet you, Joy," Andrea said. "I'm Andrea and you've now met Emily.

Once Andrea took the pizza, Joy crouched in front of Emily. "Wait until you have some of my aunt's cooking, Emily." Do you like macaroni and cheese?"

"I really like it!"

"Well, my aunt Janet makes the best I've ever tasted." Joy stood up.

"So, you made the pizza *and* delivered it? Hope someone is minding the shop."

"My mom and sister are holding the fort, but I'd better get back. Nice to meet you." Joy's eyes widened as she looked behind Andrea. "Hey there, Kyle. Long time no see. How're things?"

"Getting better, Joy. Say hi to your mom and Cathy from me." Kyle retreated with the pizza.

Joy leaned in and spoke quietly. "He's the best catch in the area. My sister tried and failed. Good luck!"

The two women grinned at each other.

"When do you get time off?" Andrea saw a single gold band on her wedding finger. "Any kids?"

"I have a daughter about Emily's age. My aunt thought we might want to arrange some play dates."

"Sounds like fun. Let's work on it." The two exchanged phone numbers.

"I HEAR YOU'RE CONSIDERED THE BEST CATCH around these parts. That true?" Andrea tried to hide a smile and couldn't. They were all sitting around the kitchen table as the large pizza did a gradual disappearing act.

Kyle blushed with a mouthful of pizza. He chewed on without speaking for a long moment. "Think I need that beer, now."

Andrea chuckled. "I did it again. I'm sorry, I made you blush."

"And then reminded me of the fact." Kyle took another bite as his color returned to normal. "Stick the knife in a little further why don't you?"

Andrea grinned at him. "You really look like you're suffering."

"Mommy, what's this green stuff?" Emily was poking the offending item towards the edge of her plate.

"It's green pepper, Peanut. You like it." Andrea turned her head to look at Emily. "It's really good on pizza. Look, Simon has eaten all of his piece."

"Okay, I'll eat it."

"That's my girl. After we're finished we can go and see what's in the backyard." Andrea winked at Kyle and went over to get a beer from the fridge. "I think there's a surprise there from our landlord."

"I'm finished. Can we go now?"

"How about you finish that piece and then we'll go." Andrea tilted her head and raised her eyebrows. Emily dutifully took another bite as Kyle took a pull of his beer.

OH, MOMMY. IT'S JUST LIKE WE HAD AT HOME." Emily ran towards the swing set and climbed on a swing, with Simon running as fast as his little legs would carry him.

"Simon, wait and let me help you." Andrea had a tray with coffee mugs and a plate of cookies. The pizza was history. Kyle's half-finished beer sat on the counter.

"I'll help him." Kyle held the door open and then trotted over to Simon as the boy narrowly missed getting hit by Emily's swing. "There you go. Hold on tight and I'll help you swing."

Andrea looked on as Kyle took turns pushing Emily and Simon. She put the tray down on the small patio table and poured two mugs. She added milk to both and carried them over towards Kyle.

"Here you go. Just the way you like it."

"Just drinking a decent cup of coffee has changed my life for the better." Kyle sipped the coffee and used one hand to keep the swings going. He was rewarded with calls to go higher and higher.

Andrea shook her head slightly. Two tired and excited children was a recipe for a tumble. She had enough family in the hospital.

"My arms are starting to hurt. I think we've had enough swinging for tonight." Kyle stopped and the swings gradually slowed their arc. "I'm going to sit with my coffee. You guys play, okay?"

Andrea smiled her gratitude as they sat down. Simon immediately plopped down on the grass on his back, looking up at the sky. Emily came over to get a cookie.

"You can bring one for Simon, too."

"That was fun, Kyle." Emily waved to him as she walked off.

"What time do you want to start the garage sale run?"

Andrea looked up in surprise. "You mean you want to come with us?"

"If it's okay with you, yes. I haven't taken a day off in a long time and never with such a pretty lady."

"Now, you're making me blush." Andrea offered him a cookie. "I'd like to get going by eight."

"I'll be here. We'll have to take your van. The truck can only carry three passengers." Kyle took a bite of the cookie. "Hmm. This is good!"

Andrea grinned at him. "Devin and Carol let me loose in their kitchen. I did a bit of baking. I actually remembered to put in all the ingredients."

"Do you make anything besides cookies?" Kyle grinned back.

"I do. If you drive tomorrow I might be convinced to invite you back for supper. It won't be fancy but it'll be filling."

"Sounds like a good deal. I'll dust off my tux."

"And I shall bring out my triple strand of pearls."

They were both smiling at each other as Emily and Simon ambled back to join them.

"MOMMY? I LIKE KYLE. He's really tall, like Uncle Richard." Emily was tucked into her bed with her teddy bear. "Is he coming to play tomorrow?"

Andrea smiled and tenderly stroked her sleepy girl's soft hair. "Yes, sweetie. He's coming with us. We're going treasure hunting tomorrow. So, you need to get to sleep."

"Good night, Mommy. Good night, Teddy." She snuggled down as Andrea laid a loving hand on her small shoulder and reached with the other to turn off the bedside lamp. "I like our new house."

"So do I, sweetie. Sweet dreams." Andrea left the room and pulled the door almost shut.

"I'M AMAZED AT HOW EASILY THEY BOTH SETTLED DOWN." Andrea smiled as she walked into her living room and found Kyle stretched out full length in the recliner. "I was expecting one or both of them to act out, especially after being spoiled by Carol and Devin for so long. And then there's Gordie, the new puppy."

Kyle sat up. "I'd best get going. Need to have an early start if I'm to be here by eight."

"You sure you want to troll for treasure with us tomorrow?"

"I'm sure. I feel like the lights are coming on in my life again. I haven't smiled this much in years." He stood and gave a little stretch. "Probably haven't talked this much in years, either."

"Well, I'm thrilled to be the one who is helping you along. I'm one of those people who always needs a project or two." She smiled up at him.

"So, now I'm a project, am I?"

"One of the best projects in a long, long time." Andrea looked at him sideways as they made their way to the front door.

"You ever been known to kiss one of your projects?"

"No. But, I think I'm about to." Andrea looked up. Even with the door open and the porch light glowing it was hard to see into his blue eyes. She raised her hand up to touch his cheek, which was sporting a fine stubble.

Kyle tucked a finger under her chin and leaned down to kiss her. Andrea shuddered at the sweetness in his light touch. As his arms went around her in a gentle embrace, she relaxed.

"See you at eight, Andrea." Kyle stepped away from her.

Andrea smiled at him. "I think I'm going to like this project."

CHAPTER TEN

ANDREA AND KYLE HAD JUST BROUGHT IN THE LAST TREASURE from a morning of checking out garage sales when her phone rang. "Hello—Oh, hi Louise—Great! Sure, I'll meet you there.

"Excuse me." Andrea shepherded Emily and Simon into the living room and settled them in with their toys and then came back to the kitchen. "I need to call Janet. Big change of plans. Then I'll make us some lunch."

"Tell me what you want to eat and I'll get things started," Kyle said.

Andrea pulled some packages out of the fridge and handed them to Kyle. Then she called Janet.

"I just got a call from my sister-in-law. She's arriving late this afternoon. Is there any chance you could babysit for a few hours? I need to meet her at the hospital and I don't want to bring the children." Andrea looked at the matched pair of Winnie-the-Pooh lamps on her kitchen table and mentally crossed her fingers.

"I had plans for this evening but I'm sure I can change them. This sounds very important. What time?"

Andrea breathed a sigh of relief. "If you could be here by four that would be great. I'll get their supper started if you don't mind presiding over the table. I'll grab something at the hospital."

She watched Kyle opening her cabinet doors looking for dishes and walked over to the right one and opened it for him. They smiled at each other.

"Thanks so much, Janet. I didn't mean to ask for emergency babysitting before you officially start." Andrea said goodbye. .

"Sorry, Kyle. It looks like my plans have all changed. We'll have to take a rain check on dinner, and to make things worse, my mother- and father-in-law are arriving tomorrow. Much as I hate the thought, I have to meet with them. I need to find babysitting for tomorrow as well."

Andrea ran a hand through her hair as she stood with the other on her hip. "I have no idea what to do. Val and her friends, including Janet and Forbesia, my back-up sitter, are all going on a Sunday afternoon tour somewhere."

"You can leave them with me at the farm," he said. "I really don't mind. Maybe I can show Simon how to pee like a boy so he can get out of diapers."

Andrea laughed. "I hadn't even thought of that part of his potty training. I'm missing the key part for demonstration purposes."

Andrea opened the fridge door to bring out some apple juice to go with the sandwiches Kyle had assembled. "I don't think I have any choice but to take you up on your offer for tomorrow. Will your father mind, do you think?"

"It will do him good to be around children," Kyle said. "Trust me, beneath that curmudgeonly crust there is a good heart. Before my mother died, I had a wonderful but shy father. I know he's still in there. Maybe Emily and Simon can help him come out."

"Do you mind practicing your babysitting skills now, while I go have a shower and get ready?"

Kyle's eyes flew open in surprise as the color crept up his neck yet again. "You expect me to watch over your children when I know you're naked in the shower back there?"

"Sorry, that's as good as it gets, for now." Andrea chuckled and walked down the short hall. *I didn't mean to go so far so fast,* she thought, *but I just love when he blushes.* She hummed to herself as she turned on the faucets and took off her clothes.

Kyle could hear Andrea moving about in her bedroom when the doorbell rang.

"Hello, Janet. C'mon in. I think Andrea is just about ready. Let me take you out back and introduce you to Emily, who is called Peanut, and Simon."

"Kyle Sheridan. You sure move fast." Janet looked around with interest as she stepped into the apartment.

Kyle laughed. "It's not the way it looks, Janet. You know Andrea got the call out of the blue. I just happened to be here to take over while she got ready."

Janet smiled. "Where are my new charges?"

"Right this way, ma'am." Kyle led the way to the shady back-yard. On this scorching hot day, the mature trees in the yard were providing welcome cover. "Can I get you a glass of lemonade?"

"Already know your way around the kitchen, too." Janet smiled. "Later is fine. I'd like to connect with the children before Andrea leaves."

"Peanut. Simon. Come and meet my friend Janet." He led the way to where a sandbox now held pride of place on one side of the yard. "We found the sand box this morning at a garage sale. We were going to go back for the play structure Andrea bought. I'll pick it up on the way home."

"Emily and Simon, this is Mrs. Henderson. She's going to be taking care of you tonight while your mom is visiting your aunt and uncle at the hospital."

Janet crouched in front of the two children and smiled at them. "I have grandchildren but they live far away. I'm hoping to adopt you as my special grandchildren, if it's okay with you," she said. "I have two dogs who would just love to have someone to play with."

"Where are your dogs? Can I see them?" Emily reached out to touch Janet's hair. "Your hair is pretty."

"Thank you!" Janet stood up and let out a small groan. "Too much gardening this morning."

"Are you the lady who made the muffins?"

"Yes, I am. I love to bake. Do you like to bake?"

Emily nodded her head. "Yes. We helped Flynn make muffins. It was fun!

"I have chairs you can both stand on to reach the counter. What's your favorite kind of muffin?"

"I like the cranberry and orange ones. They're my favorite."

Janet smiled. "I used to know someone else who really liked that kind. I'd be happy to make them with you." Janet saw Andrea out of the corner of her eye.

"Andrea, hello. You managed to rope Kyle in pretty quickly, young lady. Nice work."

Kyle looked at them both. "What is it with you ladies? This feels like a conspiracy to hijack Kyle."

"You're not complaining, I hope. Remember, it comes with home cooking and the odd bit of baking. And trust me," Andrea said, "some of my baking is pretty odd. Anyway, Janet, I must get going. Make yourselves at home. I should be back before nine. Visiting hours end at eight."

"Go on, dear. Hope everything goes well."

Andrea tugged Kyle away by the hand after kissing Emily and Simon. "You two be good and in bed no later than eight. Kyle, can you walk me to the front door, please?"

"Thanks again for helping me out." Andrea slipped on a sweater against the cool evening air.

"You could show me your thanks." Kyle winked at her. "I wouldn't mind."

"Me either." Andrea stood on her tiptoes and cupped his face in her hands and planted a warm kiss on his lips. "I'll call you later if it's not too late."

"LOUISE. I'M SO GLAD YOU'RE HERE." Andrea walked straight into the arms of her sister-in-law as she came through the hospital doors. "You must have been frantic with worry."

They hugged closely as Louise started to cry. "I was frantic all right. I know you were telling me everything was going to be all right, but I needed to see for myself. I couldn't come until my parents arrived. It's been hell waiting to get here."

"You're here now. Let's go see him, together." Andrea led the way to the elevators. "I have to warn you he's groggy from the morphine. But he's not in pain anymore."

"The times I spoke to him on the phone I could tell he was heavily drugged. Thank you so much for helping me. I can't imagine what your phone bill will be."

"Don't you worry about that. I have a package." Andrea and Louise walked into Richard's room together. A nurse was taking a blood sample. They waited while she finished.

"He's been having a good day today, ladies."

"Thanks, Jessica. This is Louise Meaken, my sister-in-law. She's just in from New Jersey."

"Hello, Louise."

"Hi. So, how is he doing?"

"Well, it looks like your husband will be leaving us next week. He'll be transferred to Walter Reed for rehabilitation. I'll leave you to your visit. If you have any questions, I'll be here. I just came on."

"Thank you," Louise said, and walked over and took her husband's hand in hers. "Richard, it's me, Louise. I'm here, my love."

She looked at Andrea and flashed a brilliant smile. "He squeezed my hand. He knows I'm here."

"He's usually very aware," Andrea smiled back. "Because of his pain medication he sleeps very soundly. He probably had a shot recently. We should let him sleep for a bit."

Andrea watched as Louise touched her husband's face, shoulders and arms, as if reassuring herself that he was alive.

"It's so hard to see him like this. He's always been so alive and full of energy." Her eyes filled with tears. "Do you know anything about the treatment program at Walter Reed?"

"Not really. But, we'll look it up on the internet," Andrea said. "How about we go somewhere and talk for a little while? I have a babysitter for Emily and Simon, but I need to be back by nine at the latest. And, we both need to eat. The food is quite good here."

They made their way to the cafeteria as Andrea brought Louise up to date on her life.

"I love my work with the vet. She reminds me so much of my father." She picked up a tray and ordered the soup of the day and a coffee. "Too bad there's no clam chowder, today. It's really good."

"I didn't know your father for very long but he was wonderful. I'm so glad to have known him even a short time. But what about Sean? Richard says you're filing for divorce." Louise picked out a sandwich. "He's injured and probably disabled. You can't just leave him."

They paid for their meals and looked for a table. "Louise, I love you like a sister, so please remember that. Leaving Sean is not negotiable. It's done. A lawyer is working on the papers."

"But why? He needs you more than ever. He's the father of your children." They sat across from each other. "What happened to for better or for worse?"

Andrea spooned up some of the hot minestrone soup and sipped on it. She put the spoon down and looked at Louise.

"I know I'm going to be having this discussion again, tomorrow, with Sean's parents. I don't expect they will understand, but I hope you will." Andrea opened a package of crackers.

"I'm sure Richard told you this. Sean started physically abusing me on our honeymoon. I know you've seen some of my injuries. You had to know they weren't accidents."

Louise lowered her eyes. "All right, yes, I suspected there were problems. But, I figured you would tell me if it got out of hand."

"I tried to tell both of you that our marriage was in shambles, but you both kept telling me a lot of women have it worse. Don't you remember how many times you told me to just stay out of his way when he was in a bad mood?" Andrea picked up her spoon and waved it in the air.

"You must remember that Easter when Emily was about two and I was pregnant. I had cracked ribs, for God's sake."

Louise looked away. "Richard told me not to interfere. He said he'd talked to Sean and made him promise it wouldn't happen again."

"Well, it did. Again and again and again. I've made my decision, Louise. I'm asking you to respect it." Andrea pushed the soup away and reached for her coffee.

Louise looked at Andrea and then looked away. "I'm sorry it came to this. You have my support. I won't question you again."

"Thank you." Andrea realized they both needed to move to less emotionally charged ground. "How are Shawna and Kendra?"

"They're great. Full of beans. They'll be wearing their grandparents out by now. Emily and Simon doing okay?"

"They love it here. They've visited horses, lambs, a pig and a puppy. You can stay with us if you don't mind sharing the bed."

"Thanks, but I'm at a nice little motel. My parents are paying for it. They realize money is always a bit tight with two growing children and trying to build a college fund." They finished their coffees and walked towards the elevators to go back upstairs and see Richard.

"When and where are you meeting Sean's parents tomorrow?" They were alone in the elevator.

"I'm meeting them here, at noon, when visiting hours start. Why?"

"I'll meet you in the lobby ten minutes ahead. You're not facing them alone." Louise reached out to hug her.

Andrea felt her throat constrict. "Bless you, Louise. I really need someone in my corner. And, you can verify my stories."

"And so can your hospital records, if it ever comes to that." They stepped off the elevator and made the short walk down the hall.

"With Lorna Garrett, it just might. I have no clue whether she'll try to get Emily and Simon or what she'll do." As they reached his room, Andrea saw her brother's eyes were open and focused.

"Go see your husband. I'll go look in on Sean and come back in a while. You two need time alone."

ANDREA WAS SHOCKED AT THE CHANGE IN SEAN. He was sitting up in bed with pillows tucked in around him and a dinner tray in front of him. He hadn't seen or heard her. She watched as he struggled with his food. The cast from his wrist to past his elbow meant he could only eat with one hand.

"Welcome back, soldier." Andrea couldn't help slipping into their old greeting.

He looked up and peered at her with a puzzled face. "Good to be home. Why am I here?"

"You were in an accident with Richard."

He winced. "Who is Richard?"

"My brother. Your brother-in-law."

Sean shook his head, as if trying to clear it. He looked at her, still puzzled. "Where am I?"

"You were in a car accident over a week ago. You hit your head pretty hard. No one knows yet how badly." Andrea wished

105

someone would come in. *I don't know what to tell him. I don't even know if he recognizes me*, she realized with a small chill.

"Do you know who I am, Sean?"

"You're really pretty." He smiled groggily. "And you're my wife. How about a kiss for your old man?"

Before Andrea even had the chance to think up a response, Sean's face darkened. "No. Wait. You left me. I remember now. I came to look for you. Richard came to bring me back. I was in jail because of you, bitch."

His bedside monitor suddenly sprang to life. Andrea could see his blood pressure was in dangerous territory. She backed away.

A nurse came running in. "Leave. Now!"

Andrea walked into the hallway in a daze. She heard Code Blue and Sean's room number. Two nurses rushed down the hall with a crash cart.

For brief seconds, she had seen the feral look in his eyes. The medications had stripped away any hint of a civilized veneer. She had seen the black hole of his soul. She was shivering as she made her way back to Richard's room.

AFTER A SHORT VISIT WITH HER BROTHER AND ANOTHER HUG FOR LOUISE, Andrea left the hospital. *I'm glad I brought a sweater with me*, she thought as she walked to her van.

Andrea got into her van and called Kyle. "Is it too late to call?"

She smiled when she heard his voice. With her hands-free on, she pulled away from the hospital and headed towards Laskin. She didn't know if she could properly concentrate on driving. She felt chilled to the bone though the air was balmy.

"How did it go?" Kyle's voice was warm and gentle.

"With Louise, it went fine. She understands."

"But…"

"With Sean, it tanked. He got so upset when he realized it was me, and remembered I left him, that he coded."

There was a short silence. "Did he survive?"

"Yes." Andrea couldn't bring herself to add 'unfortunately'.

"Guess they won't want you visiting too often."

"Guess not." Andrea was driving along the same road where she had fallen asleep and gone into the ditch. "I need to get home and see the children. Put this out of my mind."

"I can come over, if you like. Do you want a bit of adult company?"

Andrea looked at the clock on the dashboard. Just after eight. She finally shook her head. "No, but thanks. I definitely want to take you up on that offer. Just not tonight."

"The offer is open any time, Andrea."

"Thank you, Kyle. Right now, you feel like a big brother. And I don't want to feel that way about you."

"Good. Because the thoughts I'm having are nowhere near brotherly."

Laughter bubbled up as Andrea caught Kyle's drift. "You are so bad."

"And you like it, right?"

"I do. I really do." She was still smiling when she got home, the episode with Sean relegated to the back of her mind.

"Everything go well?" Janet met her at the door.

"No, but Kyle is such a character. He has just the sense of humor I needed to get through this evening."

"It's pretty clear he's soft on you." Janet said.

"That's not what he told me." Andrea grinned.

"Okay, I don't need to know any more. I'll just say good night and see you Monday."

"Thanks so much, Janet. I'll tell you all about it over coffee on Monday."

"You'll keep it clean though, right?"

"I promise." They grinned at each other.

She watched as Janet drove off. *Kyle said just the right things to help me come to grips with what happened at the hospital tonight,* she thought. *That's the kind of man I need in my life.*

She looked in on her sleeping children and then went to bed. As she snuggled into her pillow, the comforting sound of Emily's small snores reached her ears.

CHAPTER ELEVEN

ANDREA SHEPHERDED EMILY AND SIMON INTO THE SHERIDAN KITCHEN JUST AFTER TEN. "Why are you here, Janet? I thought you had other plans."

Janet smiled at her confusion. "There's been a slight change of plans. I'm going to take care of the children while you and Kyle face down your mother-in-law. At the same time, I'm going to cook up a dinner and some other things and give these Sheridan men some home-cooked meals.

"Em would have my hide if she knew how you've been eating, with me being so close by." Janet fixed Tom Sheridan with a look that brooked no argument.

Andrea looked at Tom and smiled. He looked downright uncomfortable. His hair was a mess; his clothes were shabby and his socks had holes in them. Faced with the perfectly-coiffed Janet Henderson with her pearl earrings and brightly-colored dress, he looked miserable.

"I have a feeling things are about to change in this house." Andrea watched as Simon ran to Janet and reached for her hand. "Janet, thanks so much for helping with the kids today. I need a couple of champions. The next few hours won't be easy."

Andrea looked at them. "Between you, Kyle, and Louise, I feel I have a winning team. I wish Carol and Devin were here, too. But, they're in Boston for the weekend."

Tom looked around and spoke quietly. "Andrea, I hope things go well for you, today."

Andrea looked at him in surprise and then smiled. "Thank you, sir. I really appreciate it."

"Please, call me Tom." He smiled hesitantly at her.

"Dad, we should get going. Maybe you'd like to take Emily and Simon to meet Portia?"

"Who's Portia?" Emily looked up at Kyle.

"Portia is just about the biggest pot-bellied pig you've ever seen. She's a big old gentle giant, just like my dad. She's in a pen behind the barn."

Janet chuckled. "I'd like to meet Portia, too. But not today, thank you. I'm really not properly dressed for the occasion.

"Go on, you two. Do what you have to do at the hospital and come back here for dinner. Right, Tom?"

Tom scratched the side of his forehead and stood up. "Sure. C'mon Emily, Simon. Let's go see Portia."

As they left the house, Tom looked at Kyle. "Good luck, son. She's special."

"Thanks, Dad. And so is Janet. You might want to think about that."

"She's a good cook. Not hard to look at, either."

Both men smiled nearly identical smiles.

"I DON'T KNOW IF I'M READY FOR THIS." Despite the warm sunshine, Andrea felt shivers go up and down her arms as they entered the hospital parking lot. "I'm glad you're driving. My mind is swirling. Oh, look. There's Louise. Pull over.

"Louise, hi! Perfect timing." They pulled up beside her. "Louise, this is my friend Kyle Sheridan. Kyle, my sister-in-law, Louise."

"Hello, pleased to meet you." Louise gave Kyle a little wave. "I'm parked over there. There's some spots near it. It's the blue Toyota."

"Andrea, you can get out here. I'll go park and join you."

"Thanks." Andrea stepped out of the truck and hugged Louise. "I'm so nervous. I hate confrontations. I'm afraid this is going to be a big one."

"Your friend and I will be with you. I'm sure Lorna will be civil with witnesses around."

"About Kyle." Andrea looked over to where he was now making his way towards them. He was dressed in casual slacks and an open-necked golf shirt. *He doesn't look like a farmer today.* "I'm hoping he'll be more than a friend one of these days."

"What? You haven't wasted any time." Louise stared at Andrea. "You've been here how long?"

"Two weeks and we're just friends, really. But I feel like I've known him for years." Andrea blushed when she remembered their phone conversation hours earlier. "We've only kissed twice."

Louise was about to retort when Kyle joined them. "Here we are ladies, the three musketeers. One for all and all for one."

Andrea's smile froze. "And there they are. Just walking in the entrance. Oh God, I feel so cold."

"You want to walk around a bit and work off some adrenaline? We're early." Kyle put an arm around her shoulder.

"That's a very good idea." Andrea shivered in the warm breeze. "Let's check the flower beds."

They walked around for fifteen minutes before entering the hospital lobby. Andrea was oblivious to the riot of spring colors around her and the touch of Kyle's hand at her back. She barely registered the steady stream of people going into the building with flowers and gifts.

As they approached the front door, Andrea took a couple of steadying breaths. She felt more in control and focused. They had no sooner gone through the doors than she heard her name called out.

Turning towards the sound, she swallowed hard and pasted on a small smile. "Lorna. You remember Louise, Richard's wife. And this is Kyle Sheridan. He drove me here. Louise and Kyle, this is Lorna Garrett and her husband Fred."

The men shook hands briefly but didn't speak.

"Have you been up to see Sean yet?"

"No, I have not." Lorna looked at Louise and Kyle. "You'll have to stay here. Only immediate family is allowed to visit."

Andrea looked at her in-laws, her lips pursed. "Louise and Kyle can stay in the hall. I'm sure no one will mind. We won't be staying long."

Lorna stiffened. "There are things I would like to discuss with you in private."

"There will be no more private discussions, Lorna. The one we had the other day was more than enough. I know quite well what you think of the situation and what you think of me." Andrea turned and walked towards the elevator.

As they all waited at the elevator, Lorna turned on Andrea. "You will not get custody of my only grandchildren. Grandparents have rights, too."

"Of course you do. But, I'm sure my lawyer has quite enough evidence of physical and emotional abuse that I will be given full custody. You'll have visiting rights." Andrea didn't want to be on the same elevator with Sean's mother, but she had little choice. When the doors opened, she stepped in and turned around. Her face betrayed no emotion, even as her insides churned.

"By the way, you may be in for a bit of a shock when Sean sees me." Andrea said nothing more. As they got off the elevator, she led the way.

He was asleep when they walked in. For a brief instant, his soft snoring reminded her of Emily. *She has his fine features and small nose,* Andrea thought and watched his mother step forward to kiss his cheek.

His eyes flew open. His mother stepped back and knocked into the chair by the bed. "Sean, it's me, Mom. It's okay, sweetheart. We came as soon as we could. Your dad's here, too."

Andrea had seen the look in Sean's eyes when they opened.

"Don't touch me." Sean turned his head slowly towards his mother. "I can't stand to be touched."

"I'm sorry, dear. I didn't know." She looked at Andrea, questioningly.

Andrea could only shake her head. "I have no idea what's happening."

Sean turned at the sound of her voice and snarled. "What's she doing here? Get her out of my sight. She's the reason I'm in here."

Just at that moment, Andrea saw the restraints on Sean's wrists. She raised her eyebrows but said nothing and walked out into the hall.

Kyle and Louise were standing a few feet away. "I'm going down to the nursing station. They have him in restraints. I need to find out what that's all about."

A nurse was walking towards her. "Excuse me, can you help me, please? It's about my husband, Sean Garrett in Room 405."

"You'll have to ask the nurse on the desk. I'm not one of his nurses." Andrea didn't see the scowl on the nurse's face as she walked past her.

"Thank you." Andrea went to the desk and recognized one who had cared for Richard. "Hello, Jessica. Can you tell me why my husband is in restraints, please?"

The nurse looked up and smiled. "Hi, Ms. Garrett. Unfortunately, your husband became very agitated this morning. An orderly was helping him get set up for breakfast. He didn't like what he saw on the tray and sent it crashing to the floor.

"When the orderly touched his arm to try and calm him, your husband shoved him so hard the man fell and hit his head."

"Oh my, no." Andrea paled. "Is he all right?"

"Two stitches and a headache. He's off for the rest of the day."

"Will my husband be charged?" Andrea felt rather than saw Kyle come up behind her.

"No. It's rare that a patient is charged, especially one with head injuries. We see this fairly regularly and record the behavior. It will help his rehab team understand his issues."

"Have you any word on when he'll be transferred?" Andrea smiled up at Kyle when he put his hand on her shoulder and rubbed her cheek against it.

The nurse's eyebrows went up. "Your *husband* will be transferred to Walter Reed within the next two to three days. They specialize in brain injuries."

Andrea ignored the nurse's pointed emphasis. "My brother is being transferred there, as well. It's among the top hospitals for both of their injuries. Thank you for your help." They walked back towards Sean's room.

"How's it going with his mother?" Kyle rubbed his thumb over the back of her neck.

"I think she's shocked by the change in him. She hasn't seen him for over a year. His character has really changed for the worse. I don't know whether it's the drugs or the brain injury, but he makes no effort to be civil."

Andrea left Kyle in the hall and went back into Sean's room.

She motioned for Lorna to come away from the bed and took her out into the hall. "You saw the restraints?"

"I did. What happened?"

Andrea could see that Lorna didn't like having to depend on her for information. "He assaulted an orderly because he didn't like his breakfast tray. The man went home with stitches in his head."

"Sean hates being pinned down. Been like that since he was a baby." Lorna twisted a tissue in her hands. "He'll go crazy if he's tied down. Don't know why I'm telling you that now. You're leaving him anyway."

"They don't have a choice, Lorna and neither do I." Andrea was trying to stay calm and focused. "I know it's a shock, but this is not the son you raised or the kind of man I thought I had married. I have to keep Emily and Simon safe from the danger he poses, just as the hospital has to protect its staff. Do you understand?"

"Well, he'll just cause more problems if they keep him tied down like that." Lorna refused to respond to Andrea.

"Look. What do you want me to do? I don't make the rules and neither do you. One of the staff was injured because Sean wasn't restrained." Andrea raised her hands in frustration. "Lorna, they're trying to help Sean. And, if that means tying him down then that's what they have to do. Surely you can understand that."

Andrea sighed and watched her mother-in-law deflate before her eyes. She put an arm around her tentatively and hugged her. "We've never been very close, but we're both mothers and this is your boy. I'm sorry but he's changed and his life has changed."

When Lorna looked at Andrea, there were tears in her eyes. "He's never coming home is he?"

Andrea shook her head. "I don't think so. He's being transferred this week to Walter Reed for physical and social rehabilitation. From the little I've learned, he has a very, very long recovery ahead of him. His military career is probably finished."

"I owe you an apology, Andrea." Lorna dug around in her purse for another tissue. "When I learned about the accident and his injuries, I lost it. Then, when I learned you were divorcing him, I lost it all over again." She dabbed at her eyes and blew her nose.

"I won't go after custody of Emily and Simon. But, I would like to see them before we go back to Canada. Would you mind?"

"Of course not! You're their only real grandmother. We'll stay in touch on Skype, and I'll keep sending you pictures and updates. You'll always be their Nana."

Lorna sniffled and looked over at her son, who was now talking with his father. "Will you handle all his affairs, or do you want us to take over? You'll be selling the house, I imagine."

"Yes, I will. I have a medical power of attorney and a general one. They were set up before he first deployed. I can look after that end of things. My lawyer in Boston can help me navigate, and I have a contact who is a retired social worker. She's offered to help, as well."

"Sounds like you've already built a network here."

"I have. I have a great job and some new friends. Emily and Simon love it here, too."

"I'd better go back. Fred isn't very good at conversation unless I'm there to help him."

"One more thing, Lorna. If Sean gets well enough to be released, he will need help. Would you plan for him to come and live with you?"

"I can't say at this point. Maybe yes, maybe no. It would depend on a lot of factors. One being that I'm not getting any younger."

Andrea looked at the clock. "How about if I go now and see Richard? Would you like to come for dinner tomorrow and have a visit with Emily and Simon?"

"I would like that, yes."

Andrea scribbled down her address and phone number. "I'll be off work by four. I could have something ready by five. Give me a call, and I'll give you the directions. They're really easy from here."

"Thanks, Andrea. Thank you for understanding a mother's fears and worries."

"No thanks necessary. I'd be the same."

Andrea found Kyle lounging against a wall, looking up at the ceiling. She started chuckling when she noticed that each person who went by also looked up at the same spot on the ceiling.

"Entertaining yourself?"

"Yes." He smiled and took her hand. "How'd it go?"

"I almost think we could be friends." Andrea realized with wonder. "She understands I can't live with her son any longer. She just wants to go on being Nana to Emily and Simon. She's coming over for dinner tomorrow!"

"All that worrying for nothing."

"Not for nothing. You saw her downstairs. And you didn't hear her diatribe against me on the phone. She apologized for that. That's when we turned the corner." Andrea led the way into Richard's room.

"Hello there, Ricky." She leaned in and kissed him on the cheek. "You're looking great, today! Notice how he improves the minute his wife turns up?

"Brought a new friend to meet you. Richard Garrett, I'd like you to meet Kyle Sheridan. He has the farm next to Carol and Devin."

"The one up on the hill? Great spot. Good to meet you, man." They shook hands."

"You too, Richard," Kyle said.

"So, sis, they tell you I'm being airlifted back to New Jersey this week?"

"Sean too. Maybe you'll be on the same medevac." Andrea decided against telling her brother about the deterioration in Sean's behavior.

"That would be cool. Have our stretchers side by side."

"Sean will probably be sedated for the flight." Andrea figured they wouldn't take any chances on him assaulting one of the attendants while they were in the air.

"How's he doing, anyway?"

"About the same as you." Andrea looked at Kyle. "How about we go now and let you and Louise have some time together? I'll come back and see you before you're shipped back to Jersey."

"Okay, sis. Nice to meet you, Kyle. Thanks for taking care of my little sister today."

"Sure, Richard. Hope we meet again when you're up on your feet. Just do what they tell you. Rehab's a pain, but it works."

ANDREA AND KYLE STROLLED HAND IN HAND THROUGH THE PARKING LOT, basking in the warm afternoon sunshine, the smell of hyacinth wafting through the air.

"You've been in rehab?" Andrea looked up into Kyle's face, admiring again his soft blonde curls.

"I fell off a ladder when I was fifteen. Was in the hospital for a month, but they had me up two and three times a day doing exercises with weights and physiotherapy. PT they called it. Pain and Torture." Kyle unlocked the doors. "Wonder how things are going at home."

Andrea looked at her watch. "They should both be down for a nap by now. That will give your dad and Janet a nice break."

"What are your plans for the rest of the afternoon? It's still early."

"Well, I just happen to know of an empty apartment in downtown Laskin. We could relax there for a bit and see what happens." Andrea reached over and pulled on his earlobe.

"Ouch. Okay. I give in. I'll do anything you ask." Kyle laughed and leaned over to tickle her in the side until she let go of his ear.

AT THE SHERIDAN FARM, JANET HAD JUST PUT THE CHILDREN DOWN FOR A NAP. "My this house is quiet with those two asleep, I'd forgotten how much noise and energy two little ones have."

She brought a tray of lemonade on the verandah and set it on a wicker-edged table. "This was always the place for Em and I to take a break when the last pies were in the oven. There's always a breeze."

Tom sat down in his usual chair, the shabby clothes replaced by his Sunday best. His hair was neatly trimmed.

"You still clean up pretty good, I'll give you that." Janet poured two tall glasses of lemonade and added a slice of lime to each. "Glad I remembered the lime."

"Thank you for coming over, Janet," he said. Tom picked up an icy glass and took a long swallow. "Kyle was really worried about Andrea facing her mother-in-law alone."

"He's turned into a fine young man, Tom. You must be very proud."

"I am. He stuck with me through Em's illness and refused to leave after she died. He runs the place, now. He changed us over from beef to sheep and goats because they're more sustainable."

"Looks like he's very interested in young Andrea." Janet sat back in the chair and let the breeze fan her face. "He's really come alive in just the past week or so, compared to the last time I saw him."

"She's good for him, that's for sure," he said, "Good for me, too. Kyle finally washed the kitchen floor."

"What, you don't wash floors?"

"That was always Em's kitchen. I ran the farm, she ran the house. It was like that for thirty-five years."

Janet smiled at him. "You're not running the farm now, are you? Seems to me you should do some housework and not leave it all to Kyle. He can't do it alone."

"You're right." Tom finished the lemonade and cupped his work-worn hands around it. "I was burnt out and depressed. There was nothing I could do for Em. It killed me to see her wasting away before my eyes. But, the world wouldn't stop, and Kyle was still in university in Boston."

"You could have asked for help then and any time since." Janet offered more lemonade.

"Just too proud, I guess." He held out his glass.

"Well, there's no turning back now, my dear man. You have let me into this house, and I intend to come back."

"I was hoping you'd say that."

They fell into an easy silence and watched fat bumblebees flying from flower to flower in the border in front of them. From the kitchen, came the aroma of roasting chicken and vegetables. A rhubarb crisp was cooling on the counter.

ANDREA REACHED OUT TO RUN HER FINGERS THROUGH KYLE'S CURLS. "I've been dreaming of doing this since I first laid eyes on you."

"And, I've been dreaming of this for at least the past few days." Kyle put an arm around her as she snuggled up against him in her bed.

"Do you think your dad and Janet might become an item?"

"Anything's possible. They've known each other since before I was born. My mother and Janet were best friends. Why do you ask?"

"I guess it was the way Janet walked in and took over this morning."

"Well, she knows the house and the kitchen well. When I called her last night to ask if she'd help so I could be with you, she had me open every cupboard to tell her what was in it." Kyle gave a short laugh. "Then she dictated a list of what she wanted me to go and buy and made me call her back so she could tell me what cupboard to put it in."

Andrea turned on her back and laughed. "I can just see you taking orders from her."

"When she came in this morning, she had her apron with her and some rubber gloves. Before you arrived, she scrubbed the kitchen down. I thought it was pretty clean, but it clearly didn't meet her standards."

"Have you been in her house, lately? It's spotless and gorgeous."

"I haven't been there since her husband's funeral. That was about five years ago, I guess. About a year after my mother died. I remember it was elegant. Not really a farm house the way ours is."

"What did her husband do?"

"He was a real estate developer. Made a pile of money in the eighties and nineties, but they lived very simply. They both came from humble beginnings."

"Well, speaking of your father and Janet, we'd best get going. We don't want to hold up dinner." Andrea watched in appreciation as Kyle rose up from the bed, his lean farmer's body rippling with hardened muscles.

"Hope we can figure out ways to carve more personal time in this room." She grabbed her bathrobe before heading to the shower. "If you want to share the shower, now's the time."

CHAPTER TWELVE

As they drove back to Kyle's house, they took turns telling each other stories about their lives before they met. Ahead of them, the late afternoon sun peeked in and out in a sky dappled with wispy white clouds. As they turned up the driveway, they were met by Rosie, who wagged her tail at the sight of Kyle's pickup.

"Hi Rosie," Kyle said, as he got out. "Guess you're looking for your dinner.

"I'll just put her food out and be right back."

Just minutes later, Kyle held the door open for Andrea as they came in from the mud room. "Wow, it smells good in here!"

"Sunday roast chicken. What a treat!" Andrea walked over to where Emily was putting some cut vegetables onto a sectioned plate. "What're you up to, Peanut?"

"Gamma told me to put each vegetable in its own little cup, like this." She took a handful of broccoli and put it in the cup next to the carrot sticks. "It looks pretty, doesn't it?"

"It sure does." Andrea kissed the top of her head and went off to find Simon.

She found him in the living room sitting on Tom's lap, telling him in his baby words about the pictures in his book about little dragons. It was a scene right out of Norman Rockwell. She smiled and thought of how her father would have loved to been able to read to his grandson.

She felt a little catch in her throat. "Hi, Simon. I'm back!"

Simon looked up at her but didn't move from his comfortable perch. "Hi, Mommy."

"Almost time to wash up for dinner, big guy." Andrea went over to the windows and looked out. A swing bench sat off to one side, flanked by sturdy pine side tables. *That would be a lovely spot to sit on a warm evening,* she mused. She turned back to look around the room. *It could use a good coat of paint and some new curtains, or maybe just blinds to keep out the summer heat.*

She was pulled from her reverie by Janet calling them all to the table. "Let's go, Simon. Time to wash up.

"You're looking quite dapper, Tom. Putting on your Sunday best?"

Tom smiled. "Couldn't let Janet think I don't have any decent clothes. Besides, I always dress up for company."

"Well, you look quite fine, Sir Tom."

The two children were soon seated, and Janet delivered a large platter of sliced chicken to the table. Andrea came behind with a tureen of potatoes and another of mixed beans and carrots. Kyle brought a basket of rolls.

"Janet, you have outdone yourself." Kyle offered her a roll.

"Just leave room for dessert," she said, and took one and passed the basket to Tom, who was just across from her. "I stewed a bunch of rhubarb. It's in a large container if you want some for breakfast. I'm taking some to Andrea's too. There was a lot in that patch out back."

The conversation centered on the surprise turnaround of Andrea's mother-in-law.

"I would never have believed she'd change her tune after the nasty things she'd said to me." Andrea poured some thick gravy over her potatoes and chicken. "She actually apologized. They're coming to my place for dinner tomorrow evening."

"I'll look around your kitchen and get something organized so you don't have to rush when you get home." Janet smiled at Andrea. "I'm so pleased to be around children again. They keep you young."

"I must get something to thank Val for all she's done for me, especially for recommending you to care for Emily and Simon."

"If you haven't been to Flynn and Carol's store, that's where you'll find something. Flynn knows what Val likes. He'll find you something she'll adore."

Andrea observed the way Janet was coddling Tom. Nothing overt or flirtatious. Offering him seconds. Passing the platters to him before anyone else. *She's making him feel like the lord of the manor again,* she thought with a quiet chuckle.

And Tom was loving it. He sat straight and squared his shoulders. He gave Simon things to eat from his plate and shared his bread with the toddler. Andrea sat back and smiled as she realized she could eat her own dinner in peace.

She looked over to Kyle, who was helping Emily navigate through her dinner and answering her questions about the sheep. He caught her looking at him and winked.

"JANET, AFTER THIS AMAZING DINNER, Kyle and I will take over the clean-up. You stay put." Andrea started bringing dishes to the sink as Kyle scraped and rinsed.

"Did you see the way Janet was spoiling my father over dinner?" Kyle said, taking a dinner plate out of her hand.

"Your dad was lapping it up. And smiling at everyone." Andrea made another trip to the table.

"I think we've found a cure for what's been ailing your father." She handed him a stack of side plates.

"It sure seems like it. Everything happens for a reason. You went into a ditch and the next thing I know my father has a girlfriend." He smiled at her. "Want to help me work Rosie for half an hour?"

"Sure! Can the children come and watch?"

"Of course." Kyle and Andrea chatted and worked their way through the dishes and kitchen cleanup.

EVERYONE HEADED OVER TO THE GATES LEADING TO THE UPPER PASTURE, where some two dozen sheep were grazing in the early evening light. A dozen lambs could be seen frolicking or grazing alongside the ewes.

Kyle led Andrea into the lower pasture with Rosie.

"Do you know any commands for working dogs?" Kyle smiled down at Andrea as Rosie looked on expectantly.

"None yet."

"Because the lambs are all new to this, I want Rosie to go easy on them." Kyle brought a piece of paper out of his pocket. "I've written down the commands you should use with her to get her to bring the sheep down to us. Have a look."

Andrea studied the list for a moment. "She knows all these commands?"

"And quite a few whistles and hand commands, as well. The hand commands – if you'll pardon the pun – come in handy when we're trying to locate a lost or trapped animal and we want to be able to listen for calls."

Kyle guided Andrea to a spot about fifteen feet from the pasture gate as the children, Tom and Janet looked on.

"Look at your list of commands and get Rosie to bring the flock to you. Remember to say her name before giving any command so she knows one is coming."

Andrea looked at the vibrating dog who was waiting like a rifle ready to be fired. She nodded her head, smiled and gave the command in a strong, clear voice. "Rosie, cast!"

The dog took off, running in a wide circle around the milling sheep and lambs. The ewes knew the drill but appeared protective of their lambs and were hesitating.

"Rosie, steady now, steady." Andrea marveled as Rosie immediately dropped her speed by half to give the ewes and lambs time to adjust to what was being asked of them.

"Tell her to bark. The ewes need to be reminded that she's the one in charge."

"Rosie, bark girl, bark." As Rosie continued to run, her barks had the intended effect. They all watched as the ewes and lambs began moving in the direction of the gate, a moving blanket of white and beige wool. Within seconds the entire herd was a few feet from Andrea and Kyle.

"Rosie, hold." Andrea put the piece of paper in her pocket. "Well done, girl." She walked over to the panting dog and put her hand out. This time, Rosie's tail wagged as she licked Andrea's hand.

Andrea smiled. "Hey Rosie, lie down."

Kyle smiled. Rosie had a new friend. From the gate, the children, Tom and Janet clapped. Andrea turned and gave a little curtsy.

As they walked towards the gate, Kyle spoke quietly to Andrea.

"We need to find a private corner before you leave. I need to put out some feed for the sheep and could use some help." He turned his head so the others wouldn't see his wink.

"We could go check the lambs for a few minutes. My boots are in the back of the van."

"Now you're talking."

JANET AND TOM WERE SITTING ON THE SWING BENCH with their coffees while Emily and Simon chased butterflies around the lawn.

"I'd say Kyle and Andrea have advanced to the next level," Janet said and nodded her head to where the two were huddled close together in conversation.

"What makes you say that?" Tom held his mug in both hands and looked at her.

"Andrea wasn't wearing the same clothes when they came back." Janet smiled smugly. "And she didn't say anything about spilling something and having to go home and change."

"Why, you old gossip. You should be ashamed of yourself, woman." Tom chuckled. "Leave it to you to notice."

"My mother always said the devil is in the details." Janet sipped her coffee. "Just remember that if we decide to have a good romp one of these days."

Tom sputtered. "Are you suggesting what I think you are?"

"Have you forgotten how?" She smiled, put a hand up and patted her hair. "I'm sure I can remember."

"Haven't forgotten how. Just forgotten the last time."

"Well, you have a thirty-two year old son. Tell me it hasn't been that long."

Tom reached up and scratched his head. "It was probably a year before Em died. She gradually lost interest, one thing at a time." He was quiet for a moment.

"The sex was probably one of the first to go," he said. "Then her appetite and stamina. She tried so hard for so long."

"I remember. She was still getting up and getting dressed just two weeks before she passed on." Janet patted his knee. "You took wonderful care of her, Tom. You know that."

"I did my best. She wanted to die at home. Not in some hospital bed miles away." Tom looked at her with tears in his eyes. "My Emma was so lovely. I couldn't believe it when she set her sights on me, the big, shy farmer."

"She saw the good in you. The good that's still in you and needs to get out for some fun and laughter. It's time, Tom," she said. "Keep her memory, but let her go."

"You're right," he said. "I believe it is. And I believe she would approve of you. You were her best friend."

They were both talking quietly when Andrea and Kyle walked back to the van. Andrea changed into her shoes and dumped the boots in the back before going over to see them.

"Thanks for the lovely dinner, Janet and for taking care of Emily and Simon today. See you in the morning."

Kyle helped load the children into their seats and snuck a quick kiss through the open window after closing Andrea's door.

"Would you like to come by for dinner, tomorrow? Help me with Lorna and Fred? I really won't feel comfortable alone with them, even now." She looked up at him.

"Well, if you need help with your future ex-in-laws, guess I can't say no, can I? I'll come by at half past four."

"See you then."

"Bye, Peanut. Bye, Simon." Kyle waved to them.

"Bye, Kyle," two voices chimed back.

As they were driving away, Emily said, "I like Kyle. And I like the sheep. And I like Portia. And I love the horses. It's fun here."

Andrea smiled as she pulled out onto the road. "It sure is, Emily."

"I'm going to have dinner at Andrea's tomorrow. Hope you don't mind eating alone, Dad."

"I'm going out for dinner, too. Janet invited me over." Tom had a pile of old bills and paper on the table in front of him and was sorting through them.

"She didn't invite me?"

"Nope."

"So, it's a date?"

"Could say, yes." Tom didn't see the smirk on his son's face.

126

"You rogue. One meal and you're smitten." Kyle chuckled as his father came over to set up their morning coffee. "Here, let me do that. Andrea taught me how to make a good pot."

"What's wrong with the way I make coffee?"

"Nothing, if you want to seal a roof with it."

"It's fine if you put enough milk in it." He returned to the pile of papers with a small smile playing at the corners of his mouth. "Come to think of it, we could save some money doing it your way. Go ahead. Make it your way."

As the sun set, Kyle took his coffee outside. The fireflies were just starting to sparkle in the dusk. The birdsong stopped as the sky darkened and the first stars appeared.

ANDREA WAS SITTING IN HER BACKYARD after settling the children. *My world has taken a quantum leap forward,* she reflected. *This morning, my mother-in-law despised me. I thought I was going to face her alone. My sister-in-law was against me leaving Sean. I hadn't made love in more months than I can remember. Now, I'm in love with the world and one certain man in it.*

She looked up at the stars, wrapped her arms around her knees and hugged the warm feeling in her heart.

Chapter Thirteen

The voice on the other end of the line was unfamiliar. "Andrea Garrett?"

"Yes," she said.

"This is Captain Argyle. I'm Sean's commanding officer. How's he doing?"

Andrea was stunned. "How did you get my phone number? It's new and unlisted."

"Your sister-in-law gave it to me. I was checking up on your brother's condition. I'm calling to see if you need any help. Have you spoken to Family Advocacy?"

"Thank you for calling and for your offer, but everything is under control. Sean has been diagnosed with traumatic brain injuries. He's being airlifted to Walter Reed to start rehabilitation this week. I'm told he'll likely remain there for at least a year."

"That is not good news for him or the U.S. Army." There was a short silence. "Mrs. Garrett. It has come to my attention that you are planning to divorce Sean on the grounds of physical abuse. Is that so?"

Andrea shook her head. *Military intelligence. I thought it was an oxymoron.* "Yes, I will be filing for divorce. Why?"

The captain cleared his throat. "We take great pride in our military families. I'm sure you're aware he has PTSD."

"I'm very aware. I'm also aware now that you knew it and sent him back into combat."

"He's one of our best. He wanted to be redeployed. He showed no outward symptoms."

"Except at home in front of our children." Andrea massaged her forehead. She felt a tension headache forming. "What is the purpose of your call, please?"

"I'm asking you not to make the abuse public. He'll be in rehab for months, your divorce will go through. What purpose will be served other than to air your family issues in public?"

Andrea sighed. "I certainly don't want to hit anyone when they're down. I'm listening."

"Once he's transferred to Walter Reed and fully assessed, we'll know more. If you're willing to stand by Sean, you could instruct your lawyer to change the grounds to irreconcilable differences. Would you be willing to do that?"

Andrea rubbed the back of her neck to try and ease the tension. "Let me talk to my lawyer. If he's in agreement, I will consider it, yes."

"I think you're making a wise decision, Andrea. This is not the time to make things more complicated. You and Sean have some tough times ahead and some tough decisions to make."

Her head was beginning to throb. "Thank you for your call."

Janet arrived and set down a large cooler bag and a cloth bag. "Are you all right, Andrea?"

"I have a bad tension headache." Andrea closed the front door and sat down on the couch. "Sorry, I just got off the phone with Sean's commanding officer."

Janet took off her jacket and hung it over a chair. "Could I make us some tea?"

Andrea smiled, thinly. "That would be very nice. Thanks."

"Where are the children?"

"Emily is playing in her room. Simon is still sleeping. I think yesterday wore him out." Andrea followed her, sat down at the kitchen table, and put her head in her hands. "I'm not much good when I get one of these."

"Did you take something for it?" Janet opened the cooler and brought out a glass casserole dish and set it on the stove. Reaching back in, she brought out another covered dish and set it beside its companion.

"I took a couple of pills. I'll be fine." Andrea looked up. "I'm sure the tea will help, too. You've been doing a bunch of cooking!"

Janet smiled. "I'm used to doing everything in large batches for the Sweet Repose. I've brought the macaroni I promised for lunch.

And I made beef bourguignon for your dinner tonight. Tom and I will be having the same thing."

"You've invited him home for dinner?" Andrea smiled and felt the tension easing. "You don't waste any time either."

"The Sheridan men are good people. They just need good women to remind them of the fact." Janet filled the kettle with water and turned it on. "I see you and Kyle have something happening already."

"We do. It's early days, but it feels good." Andrea stood up and lifted the lid on the still-warm beef bourguignon. "This smells heavenly. I'm starting to feel better just smelling this."

"So, what did Sean's commanding officer want?"

"He asked me to withdraw the abuse complaint. He was being extremely protective of the army's reputation."

"Can't say I blame him." Janet poured water into the teapot and put the lid on. She set the stove timer for three minutes. "The army has invested a lot of time and money in Sean's training. It doesn't excuse or explain the abuse you endured, but it does explain its position."

"I know. I've thought through all that for almost four years." Andrea put out some milk and sugar. "I agreed to withdraw the complaint if my lawyer agrees. I don't want anything to affect me getting sole custody of the children."

"What are you going to do?" Janet poured two steaming mugs of tea just as Emily came bounding into the kitchen. "Hi, Peanut. How are you?"

"Hi, Gamma. Did you bring muffins?"

"If you bring me the cloth bag near the front door, we might be able to find some."

Emily ran down the hall, her feet thumping on the old wooden floors.

"I'm going ahead with the divorce. That much, I know." Andrea stirred some sugar and milk in her tea and took a sip. "I'll have full access to health benefits for myself and the children. The court will decide the amount of support and it will be deposited straight into my bank account automatically."

She stopped talking as Emily came back in the room. "I think Simon is awake. I'll be right back."

A few minutes later, she was back in the kitchen with a sleepy Simon in her arms. "Look who's here, Simon. It's Gamma.

Simon reached out to Janet, who took him in her arms. He reached up to play with an earring.

Andrea took a long drink of her tea and looked at the clock. "Val knew I'd be a bit late this morning, but I'd better get going. I'm leaving early, too."

"Here's your lunch. I promised." Janet handed Andrea a container of her macaroni and cheese. "Say hi to Val for me."

"I will. Thanks for everything." Andrea picked up a jacket and headed out the back door. Her van was parked in a wide alley behind the building.

As she drove away, she shook her head, knowing the headache wouldn't go away any time soon.

ANDREA FELT WORN OUT DESPITE HER SHORTENED WORK DAY. As she walked in through her back gate, she smelled the beef bourguignon and quietly gave thanks for Janet. Emily and Simon ran to give her hugs as Janet looked on. After a quick update on the children's day, Janet left and Andrea was left to herself with the little ones. Kyle arrived at four thirty and was quickly set upon by Emily and Simon. Within seconds he was on backyard swing duty.

Andrea's doorbell rang promptly at five o'clock.

"Lorna, Fred. Come in, please." Andrea opened the door wide. "Kyle is out back with Emily and Simon. If you follow me, I'll take you through."

"I thought we were visiting with just you and the children." Lorna looked at Andrea. She was not smiling.

"Kyle offered to help and I agreed. I've had a very difficult day and I'm quite tired." Andrea felt her neck stiffening all over again. "I have some appetizers ready."

Lorna said nothing but followed her down the hall towards the back of the house.

"How was Sean, today?" Andrea stopped by the kitchen table to pick up a tray of vegetables and dip. "Do you mind carrying these out, please?"

"He was so sedated we couldn't really have a conversation. A nurse came by and shooed us out after half an hour. Said they had to do some tests before he's transferred."

"I don't like hearing he's heavily sedated. I'll call the hospital before you leave and see if I can find out what's going on. I'll be along in a minute. I have a plate of mini quiches warming in the oven."

AS THE ADULTS GATHERED AT HER PATIO TABLE, ANDREA FELT THE TENSION IN THE AIR as surely as the throbbing in her head. "May I offer you some wine?" Andrea prayed for her mother-in-law to down a couple of glasses of wine and loosen up a bit.

"Yes, I think I need a glass, thank you." Lorna sat quietly. When Andrea handed her a glass of Shiraz, she drank without tasting.

Emily and Simon had each been given a plate of appetizers to snack on. Andrea figured it would hold them down without needing the main course. They were now playing in the sandbox with some old toys Neil had found in his shed.

Lorna took another long sip, looked at them and finally spoke. "I'm not blind, Andrea. Your friend Kyle here is clearly more than a friend. You aren't even legally separated from Sean, and you're bedding the first man who catches your fancy? Don't you have any self-respect?"

Andrea drew in a sharp breath. "Lorna, please don't go there. I thought we had reached an amicable truce yesterday." She rubbed her forehead. "I'd like to work on that if you're willing. But, I will not have you disrespect what I am doing with my life.

"You need to remember that this is my life. I'm an adult. I'm making decisions about my life and my future that I believe are right for me and for Emily and Simon. I'm asking you to respect that." She half-closed her eyes in pain as she pushed out the last words.

Lorna gulped more wine. "I just can't believe you'd cheat on Sean when he's lying in that hospital bed, critically injured."

"I don't think it's called cheating if you're filing for divorce."

Kyle cleared his throat. "If I could get a word in here, please."

Both women stared at him. Lorna held out her glass for a refill.

Kyle addressed himself to Lorna. "Andrea has become very special to me in the past couple of weeks. She's helped me break out of my prolonged grief at losing my mother a few years ago and also almost losing my father, who couldn't get past *his* grief." He stood and went behind Andrea's chair and massaged her shoulders. "Andrea gave me back my father and gave *me* back my joie de vivre. She's very special to me and my father.

"Please Lorna, you know Andrea's a good person and a good mother. You know she's doing her best to provide a good life for Emily and Simon." He looked down at Andrea. "I believe that life should include me. I'm not perfect, but I feel that Andrea and I are kindred spirits. We love animals. We love children. And we love people."

Andrea looked at Lorna and saw her wavering as she sipped more wine. "Lorna, I'm very sorry about what has happened to Sean. I truly am, but I was never able to really connect with him. It was as if there was something lingering there behind his eyes that I couldn't reach. You must know what I'm talking about."

Lorna nodded, then she sighed and looked at her husband. Her eyes filled with tears. Fred nodded, almost imperceptibly.

"Sean is troubled," she said. "He always has been. We've never told anyone but…" Lorna's voice was quiet for a moment. Andrea had to strain to hear her. "Sean was caught more than once hurting and torturing animals. We were both horrified. We did our best to try and help him understand that all life is to be respected."

Fred coughed, put his glass down and sat forward. "It started when he was about seven. Our dog had a litter of puppies out in our equipment shed. There were six very healthy little Labs. We went out one morning and there were only five left. At first, we thought maybe a fox or coyote got one. We live in the country. But Lorna found blood and fur in a box in Sean's closet, along with a bloody knife. It had started to smell."

Lorna looked up with agonized eyes. "When he was twelve, a neighbor's cat went missing. Then another and another. They just disappeared with no trace. I didn't connect it to the puppy, but one day I found a notebook in Sean's room."

She shook her head and looked away. "There were photos. Grotesque polaroids of mutilated cats with notes on the techniques he used. I didn't know what to do or who to turn to."

"That's why you jumped away when Sean opened his eyes yesterday." Andrea sat still as Kyle's hands rested on her shoulders. "You've seen that look before, haven't you?" Andrea ignored the buzzing timer on her oven.

"Yes. When I confronted him with that notebook, he was proud of it. He called it a scientific experiment. He was recording which method could be used for the longest time before the animal died." Lorna covered her face. "I thought the army would help him reign in his urges and impulses. I never wanted anyone to get hurt, especially you, Andrea and never, ever, the children."

There was a long silence.

Andrea spoke first. "Lorna, I know you want to protect Sean. I also know the Army wants to protect one of its own, for good reason. But I think we all realize that Sean is a very dangerous man whose brain injuries could remove every last bit of civil veneer he has.

"I'm hoping you'll take your story to the Army. Combined with mine, we have to make sure he never holds a weapon again. That's all I'm hoping for. Even though we're civilians, we too have a duty to protect."

Lorna nodded tearily as her husband went to her and put his arms around her. Fred looked at his wife, who was now crying quietly. "We've been carrying this secret for over twenty years, sweetheart. It's time to stop covering for Sean. There are too many lives at stake, including Emily's and Simon's."

Lorna sobbed. Andrea reached out and put a hand over Lorna's. "Lorna, thank you. I'm so sorry, but you've done the best thing. You've taken a brave step forward, and you won't be alone when you take the next one.

"Would anyone like to eat now or shall I just put it away?"

Fred hugged his wife. "I don't think either of us is hungry."

ANDREA LET EMILY AND SIMON STAY UP A BIT LATER so that Lorna and Fred could have a visit with them. Later, the two grandparents shared bedtime duties and some story telling. Andrea used the break to call the hospital

"This is Andrea Garrett, Sean Garrett's wife… His mother told me that he was heavily sedated when she was there to visit him today. I'd like to know why, please… okay, thank you." Andrea turned receiver from her mouth and looked over at Kyle. "They're putting me through to his nurse."

"Hello, Sherry. Could you please tell me why Sean was so medicated that he couldn't speak with his parents this afternoon?" Andrea listened and sighed. "I'm so sorry to hear that… Yes. No of course, I understand now."

Andrea ended the call and shook her head at Kyle. "Whoo, boy. Sean lost it, again. I'd better get Lorna and Fred in here so I don't have to repeat myself."

Minutes later they were all gathered in the livingroom.

"Thanks for putting the kids to bed." Andrea offered a wan smile as Lorna and Fred came into the room and sat down. "Sean's restraints were removed so he could shower and shave this morning. They want him to do things for himself as much as possible."

Kyle handed her a mug of coffee.

"He seemed to be in good spirits and was cooperative, so they let him sit in the chair and eat his breakfast without any restraints." As Andrea spoke, Fred put his hand on Lorna's lap.

"Apparently, he was fine all morning," she said. "The doctor came by to check on him. His nurse checked in on him. Everything was looking good. Then, for no apparent reason, he completely lost it." Her mother-in-law moaned.

"Lorna, he assaulted his nurse. The one I spoke with was the woman who replaced her. The other one, Jessica, is in emergency with a broken collar bone from him slamming her against a wall."

Lorna put her hand in front of her mouth and shook her head. "With his head injuries, he's become so dangerous."

Andrea nodded. "From what I've read online, the TBI is affecting his ability to control his emotions and reactions. Given his past violent history, his violence is unleashed. He can no longer control himself, sober or drunk."

"Will it ever stop?" Lorna's look was pleading.

Andrea looked at her and shook her head slowly. "There's no way of knowing yet how much damage the accident caused. With his history of brain injuries, he probably won't ever be fully normal again."

Lorna looked at Fred. "I think we'd better leave. I've had all I can take for today. Thank you for inviting us, Andrea. I think we'll stay another day or two and then head home. We're on a fixed income. This trip has eaten into our rainy day savings."

"I understand. How about we meet for lunch at the Sweet Repose tomorrow? It's right next door. My treat."

Lorna smiled, but it was a dim smile. "That would be very nice. You sure you have time?"

"Family first. I know Val will understand."

As she closed the door behind them, she turned back to find Kyle gathering up the mugs. "I can do that."

"Sure you can," he said. "So can I."

"Lorna is grieving the loss of her son. As a mother, I feel for her," Andrea said and turned off a table lamp. "I can't imagine them keeping Sean's torturing of animals a secret all these years. Had I had even a tiny inkling, I never could have married him."

"Of course not." Kyle led the way to the kitchen.

"The only good to come out of this are my sleeping children back there."

When they reached the kitchen, they both put down what they were carrying and went to each other and hugged for a long silent moment. Kyle tangled his fingers in Andrea's hair as she started to cry and held her close.

"I can't believe I married and slept with a man who could torture animals. I just can't."

"Shh, Andrea. You didn't know." Kyle held Andrea's shaking body. "Focus on Emily and Simon. They are your present and your future now."

Andrea shuddered and let out a long sigh. "Thank goodness for them. And for you. Thank goodness you were here tonight. I'm so glad I'm not alone with this."

"I think I should stay the night. You shouldn't be alone."

Andrea nodded. "Yes, please."

"I'll call my dad and let him know. Can I borrow your iPhone?" He smiled sheepishly. "Guess I should buy one."

Andrea sniffled as a small smile formed on her lips. "You always know the right thing to say to lighten the mood."

THEY AWOKE TOGETHER EARLY THE NEXT MORNING TO A WARM SPRING SHOWER. Andrea snuggled up against Kyle. "Wake up, sleepyhead. You need to get back to the farm."

"If you give me a kiss, I'll help you wash up from last night."

"I owe you a major hug and kiss for all your help last night. I'm not sure I would have been able to sleep had you not been here."

"And I owe you the same for dragging me out of my shell and back into the land of the living."

"It wasn't that hard. I'm surprised someone didn't try long before this." Andrea circled an arm around Kyle's narrow waist.

"Some tried. Cathy got me out a few times."

"What happened? If she's as nice as Joy, she'd be wonderful."

"The timing wasn't right, then. Cathy is now happily married. We're still friends, although I rarely see her. You going to set up a play date with Joy and her kids?"

"Not just yet. I still haven't found any equilibrium with everything that's happening to Richard and Sean. Think I'll lay low until that gets sorted out."

"Makes sense." Kyle leaned over and planted a kiss on her head. Tucking a finger under her chin, he raised Andrea's head. They kissed for a long moment before heading down to the kitchen.

The sun was just peeking over the horizon when Kyle finished up his coffee. "Thank you for the coffee and muffins, Ms. Garrett. What are your plans for Saturday?"

"What did you have in mind?" Andrea asked.

"I thought Emily and Simon might like to come by and spend some time with the animals. You could stay for lunch, too. Make a day of it."

"How about I bring lunch?"

"That would be a real treat." Kyle gave her another quick kiss and stepped out the door.

Andrea locked it and went back to wake up Emily and Simon. As she walked down the hall, she realized she could still smell his scent around her. She stood, with her eyes closed, and breathed in the mixture of smells. It smelled like a home, at last.

CHAPTER FOURTEEN

ANDREA SLIPPED HER PHONE IN HER POCKET. VAL LOOKED OVER AT HER, They were in Val's dispensary organizing rabies, tetanus, and West Nile vaccines for many of the horse owners in the region. "Sean and Richard are both being transferred to Walter Reed tomorrow by an army medevac helicopter."

"The two buddies flying back together." Val checked the expiration date on a case of rabies vaccine. "Nice that they can go together."

"Only Richard will be awake. The nurse told me that Sean is kept sedated now and, until he's in the hands of the experts tomorrow, he'll be pretty much like he was when his mother and father visited on Monday. He couldn't converse with them."

"I'm guessing you're pretty relieved that he's going away."

"You have no idea how relieved." Andrea counted out the West Nile vaccines they'd need. "We're going to be pretty busy for the next week or so! How did you ever manage alone?"

"Ask my husband. I'm never home for most of the spring. I have no time for a vegetable garden. My house is a mess, although it's getting better now that I have your help here."

Andrea grimaced. "Speaking of that, I need a day off to go to Boston to see my lawyer about the separation papers. I also need to go to the bank and arrange for part of Sean's pay to be transferred here until the divorce goes through. One of these days, I need to go to New Jersey to pick up more of my belongings, get my Tricare file and organize to put the house on the market."

Val stopped what she was doing and peered at Andrea over her bifocals. "We both agreed that family comes first. We'll work it out. Just promise me you won't get a guilty look on your face every time you need to care for a sick child or do something for your family."

Andrea smiled. "I promise. Is there a day that's best for you?"

"I have a better idea. Let's close at noon on Fridays and leave one morning a week open, say Wednesday. What do you think?"

"You're the boss. You tell me."

"I'm asking you."

"Having Friday afternoons off would sure help. I could make a late appointment with the lawyer in Boston, assuming he's working." Andrea nodded. "Wednesday morning would work for banking, groceries and other errands. Janet could hold the fort with the kids. It would work."

"All right, then. How about you go get Lisa in here? I want to be sure this works for her, too."

Andrea returned with a woman not much younger than her.

Val topped up a box and labeled it with the contents and quantity. "Lisa, did Andrea tell you we're thinking about changing our hours?"

"She did. I think it would work out very well. I don't mind coming in Friday mornings if it means I could have Wednesday morning to myself to get a few things done."

"How old is Stephen now?"

"He'll be four in September."

"You two should get your kids together, sometime."

Lisa smiled across at Andrea. "We've been talking about organizing a play date with Joy and her two."

Andrea spoke up. "Now that Sean and Richard have been moved out, I'll have some more time to myself."

"How about this Saturday?"

Andrea shook her head and laughed. "Already taken. We're going over to Kyle Sheridan's to visit his animals and take Emily and Simon for a horseback ride."

"You're dating Kyle? I've had a crush on him since we were in high school." Lisa grinned at Andrea and then looked at Val sheepishly. "Anything I can help with here?"

"Just listen for the phone and take a break." Val smiled and checked another box for the expiry date. "How about you make a few calls later and rearrange our schedule? Let's start our new hours next Friday, if that's okay with you, Lisa."

"It should be fine. My mom looks after Stevie, and I have a back-up if she can't do it."

The three women chatted until the phone rang and Lisa went out to take the call.

"How long has Lisa been with you?" Andrea rearranged a shelf of medication boxes and dusted the shelf.

"I guess it's almost six years. She'd been with me a year when she got pregnant. Practically dropped Stevie on her desk. Went into labor in the waiting room with at least five people and their animals all looking on." Val chuckled. "One of my clients took over the phone and another one got Lisa onto that table there while we waited for her husband to come and get her. She made it to the hospital with about half an hour to spare."

"I like her. She's a spunky woman."

"You are too, Andrea." Val stretched and rotated her shoulders. "I don't know if you realize it, but every day I see new confidence coming out in you. When I first met you that day on the street with Carol, you were shocked that I would hire you, weren't you?"

"Well, you didn't know me and hadn't checked my credentials."

"But, you also didn't think you were worthy. It wasn't anything you said, it was more the way you stood. Your body language."

"I was still recovering from the concussion."

"Still, I think you've come a long way in just a few weeks. I hope you appreciate it."

Andrea smiled at Val as they packed the last of the vaccines into a cooler. "Thanks for your support, Val. I do feel stronger and more in control. Sean's accident really threw a wrench into everything, but I'm coming out the other side, now."

"So, what's this I hear? You and the kids are spending Saturday at Kyle's farm? I'm impressed. You moved fast!"

Andrea grinned. "I plied him with muffins, Janet's beef bourguignon, and a bit of Garrett love thrown into the pot. Told you, when I set my sights on someone, resistance is futile."

"Have you met Portia?"

"I did. That is one cute pig."

"My thought exactly. Smart too. Figured you'd like her." Val looked around. "All right, that's it. We're set for a few days. Why don't you go home and let's both take a break. We've both put in some long days."

"Thanks, Val. A hot shower and an early evening are starting to sound really good."

Andrea had just gotten Emily and Simon settled in for the night and was startled when her phone rang. Only a handful of people had the number. She looked at the call display and smiled.

"Hello, you!"

"Just wanted to make sure you're all coming over tomorrow."

"We are. I made up some hamburger patties for the kids. I'll pick up steaks for us, there's a couple of salads and some fresh lemonade. I saw the barbeque on the porch off the kitchen."

"Guess I know what I'm doing tonight. That barbeque hasn't been used in maybe seven years. It's probably turned into a nest, for all I know. I don't think there's any propane. Good thing I called."

"We can always use the stove. Don't go to any trouble."

"You know what? It's time I got it cleaned up and ready to use. I haven't had a good home-cooked steak in years. Any plans for Sunday dinner?" She could almost hear Kyle grin into his phone.

"This is all about food, isn't it?" Andrea smiled. "I've reawakened a bear. You're coming out of a long hibernation from good food."

"The bear is definitely awake, and food is not the only thing on his mind, I can assure you."

"What are we going to do about that?"

"You could sleep over. There are four bedrooms. My dad and I only use two of them. I could open up the other two and air them out a bit. Check for mice."

"Have you caught any?" Andrea opened up the fridge door and did a quick inventory for the next day.

"Three, so far. I found two in a drawer in the kitchen this morning. Did a catch and release on them. The other had gotten into a bin and couldn't get out. But, he must have died happy. It was organic oatmeal."

"Remind me not to have oatmeal for breakfast on Sunday." Andrea wrinkled up her nose at the thought.

"I'll make pancakes with sausages and Canadian bacon."

"You'll cook for me? Us?"

"I did live on my own for a few years. I'm pretty handy in the kitchen."

"Not that anyone could see *that* the first day we met." Andrea marveled at the changes in Kyle since that day.

Kyle's voice was soft. "My father and I isolated ourselves after my mother died. Looking back, it wasn't healthy, but we were so lost without her. She had a powerful presence."

"I know. Both Val and Janet told me. She was a very special woman from what they've told me."

"She would have really liked you, Andrea. I'm certain she would have felt you were the daughter she never had."

Andrea warmed at his words. "Val told me she loved to laugh and loved to cook and bake."

"She also liked to play practical jokes, especially on my father. When I was young, maybe ten years old, we had a bunch of newborn heifers. It had been raining solid for a week and we were all getting cabin fever. I don't know how she did it, but this one morning, my dad and I went out and here were all these heifers standing around in rain boots! She had made some mixture of flour and water, put it in the bottom of the boots and it stuck to their hooves."

"Go on. How did she do it without anyone seeing?"

"My dad tended to fall asleep in his chair after dinner. I went to bed early, too. She must have waited 'til we were both asleep."

"What did your father say?"

"He laughed until the tears streamed down his face. Then, he went and got the camera and took pictures. I still have them somewhere."

"That's hilarious. Sounds like I would have gotten along well with your mom."

"Does that mean you like to play practical jokes?"

"Wait and find out." Andrea grinned. "See you around nine?"

"Yes. And don't worry about a nightgown. I don't think you'll need one."

"I will bring a dressing gown. I don't parade around nude in front of my children."

He chuckled. "I'm really looking forward to this weekend."

"Me too. Now that Sean is gone, I feel my life is opening up to new possibilities." Andrea looked up at the clock.

"I hope those possibilities include me."

"They do, but only if I get a good night's sleep. Say goodnight, Kyle."

"Good night Kyle," he said.

Andrea grinned and shook her head as she ended the call and put her iPhone on silent for the night. She first crept into Emily's room and then Simon's room, and took out sleepers for both and more diapers for Simon.

A sleepover at Kyle's, she thought and grinned as she made her way to her room.

She opened the bottom drawer of her dresser and brought out a gossamer nightgown she'd bought in Boston, at Carol's insistence. *I didn't believe I'd ever need it, but Carol said I need to be prepared for love when it happens.*

She looked at the filmy confection and whispered, *"Thank you, Carol."*

She pulled out a small suitcase and packed everything into it, mentally reminding herself to be sure to bring along Emily and Simon's cuddlies. Climbing into bed, she took one last look at the clock. Nine hours until she was standing next to Kyle again.

She hugged her pillow and soon fell asleep.

"GOOD MORNING, YOU TWO." Kyle smiled at Simon and Emily as he opened the van door. "Did your mom tell you about my goats?"

"I want to ride the horse." Emily reached out her arms after Kyle unbuckled her seat belt.

"Me, too! Me, too!" Simon bounced in his seat, waiting to be released.

Andrea chuckled. "Stop wriggling, Simon. I'll have you out in a second."

The two children ran off towards the house as Andrea and Kyle followed at a more relaxed pace. Tom was smiling as he opened the door and welcomed the little ones inside.

"They're really excited. It could be fun trying to keep their energy under control long enough to sit up on one of the horses." Andrea took a deep breath of fresh air. Birds of all kinds were warbling in the trees surrounding the house.

"Guess we should let them run around for a while, first. Chasing the goats will help. I've put the billy in a pen for the day and also the ram. I wouldn't trust either of them around the children." Kyle peered into the cooler. "Mmm. Looks like no one will go hungry."

"Did you clean up the barbeque?"

"Yep. Good thing I checked. I won't tell you what was living in it."

"Thanks for not saying." Andrea laughed. "I picked up steaks on the way here and made enough salads to last through the weekend."

After putting away the food, Kyle picked up her suitcase and took Andrea up to see the bedrooms. "I left the windows and doors open over night. No signs of mice up here."

Andrea smiled in appreciation at the high ceilings. "This must stay reasonably cool in the summer."

"It's usually comfortable, yes. But we also have summer bedrooms out back, on the other side of the mud room. My parents put an old brass bed out there for each of us. Comes in handy on muggy nights."

Kyle led her into the smallest of the bedrooms. "This was my room when I was little, before I needed a desk, bookcase, file cabinet and printer stand. Simon can sleep in here."

He walked to the small closet and opened the door. "I remembered these yesterday."

He pulled out a square box from the back of the closet, opened it and handed Andrea a wooden train. Then he brought out a wooden bus, and a car. "These were mine when I was about Simon's age. My dad made them."

"They're perfect for a toddler." Andrea looked at the train. "There's no metal. Nothing small enough to choke him. Your dad knew what he was doing."

"I played with those things until I was about seven or eight. He made them from scraps of wood. He never painted them. Didn't want me to get sick by eating paint. There's a few more pieces in another box."

"He'll have fun with these. But, he won't want to leave them when we go home tomorrow."

"He can bring them home. They're meant to be played with, not to sit in a closet." Kyle put the toys back in the box. "Let's see Emily's room and then I'll show you mine ... ours."

Andrea looked around the larger room, noting the plush multicolored quilt adorning an antique four poster bed. She crossed the room and ran her hands over it. "Don't often see quilts like this anymore."

"This one was made by my great-grandmother after the end of World War One. It used to be on my parents' bed but my father put it in here after Mom died."

Andrea shook her head. "I guess the memory of it was too painful?"

"I didn't really think about it, but I think you're right. Think Emily will like it?"

"She'll love it. It has all her favorite colors in it," she said. "Where's my suitcase?"

"I left it in the hall."

"I'll just get it and put her things in here and put Simon's stuff in the other room. Be right back."

Kyle stood in the empty room and felt the loss of Andrea's happy energy. *I never realized how morose this house and my life had become,* he thought. *Dad and I have pined away far too long. I don't want this weekend to end.* He smiled at the thought, just as Andrea almost skipped into the room.

"Okay, here's Emily's stuff." She put the changes of clothing on top of the large mirrored dresser. "Where's your room?"

"I saved the best for last, of course. Right this way."

Kyle opened his bedroom door and stepped aside. "I cleaned it up as best I could."

Andrea was surprised by the change in décor. Where the other two rooms had a decidedly Victorian air about them, Kyle's room was modern and functional. One end of the room was set up as an office, with a large flat screen monitor, laptop and keyboard. A queen-sized bed took up only a fraction of the remaining space.

"This bedroom is huge." Andrea held out her arms and twirled around. "Not going to hit anything in here."

"This was my parent's bedroom, originally. It's the master." Kyle watched her with a smile. "You like it?"

"What's not to like?" She walked over to the bed and plopped down on it.

They both heard the sound of small feet thumping up the stairs. "Sounds like they got away from my dad."

"Sounds like. How about we get them back outside for some fresh air?" Andrea stood and together they showed the children where they would be sleeping for the night.

"OKAY, ANDREA, YOU GET UP ON TACO FIRST and I'll hand Emily up to you." Clyde and Taco were saddled up and tethered to the paddock fence. Bonnie was no longer up to riders.

Kyle swung up onto Clyde's broad back, as Tom and Simon looked on. "Dad, if you could hand Simon to me, we're all set to go."

"Watch out for skunks over in the east pasture. Smelled some yesterday."

"I'm surprised Portia hasn't scared them off." Kyle settled Simon in front of him. "Simon, remember, you need to hang on to my arm and sit still.

"We'll be back within an hour. We'll go over and say hi to Devin and Carol." Kyle turned Clyde towards the trail that would take them down the hill to the neighboring farm. The horses seemed to know where they were going and tossed their heads in anticipation.

Andrea snuggled Emily against her. "What do you think, Peanut? Are you having fun?"

"I like Taco's hair. It's thick."

"Well, you hold onto it. Just don't pull it."

They made their way slowly towards the stately Victorian down the hill. The sky was cloudless. Overhead, a pair of noisy crows were being chased by a flock of blackbirds. Butterflies flitted among the myriad field flowers while dragonflies patrolled. Andrea and Kyle chatted on the wide path.

"Do they know we're coming? Maybe we should have called ahead." Andrea could see the cars and Devin's truck were all in the driveway.

"It's Saturday. Pretty sure Devin will be around. I think I see Gregory over by the stable door." He pointed out a tall figure moving near the building entrance.

"I want to see the kitties." Emily leaned forward as Andrea tightened her grip.

"Sit back, Emily. I don't want you to fall off." Andrea looked at the scene from a new perspective. "That is such a beautiful property."

"It is. Devin is a great neighbor, too."

The little group made its way to Devin's paddock and were rewarded with Carol coming out the side entrance and waving at them.

"Thought I recognized the little riders. C'mon in. I have cookies somebody might like." Carol looked up smiling as the horses stopped. She reached up and took Emily into her arms. "Hi, Peanut. That's a really big horse you're riding."

"That's Taco." Emily put her hand in Carol's. "Can I go see the kitties? Where's Gordie?"

"Who do you want to see first, the kittens or Gordie?"

Emily stopped to think. "I want to see Gordie."

"Let's go in the house, then. He's in the kitchen." Carol took her by the hand and led her away.

Andrea took Simon off Kyle's lap and put him on the ground. "Let's go see Gordie."

"See Gordie." He nodded and pulled his mother towards the house.

"What's the story on Sean?" Carol and Andrea snagged a few minutes alone as Kyle and Devin took the wriggling puppy and children to the sun-filled solarium.

"He's been transferred to the Walter Reed medical center in Bethesda. They have an excellent trauma center." Andrea accepted a mug of freshly-made coffee. "He'll be thoroughly assessed, but I've been told it could easily be a year before they'll be able to consider what future he may have in the military."

"What are you going to do?" Carol set out a plate of cookies and poured herself a coffee.

"His commanding officer called me and asked me to withdraw the abuse as grounds for the divorce. I checked with Peter Stinson and he agrees we can cite irreconcilable differences. With Sean in rehab, I'll have full custody. He's no longer a threat to me. I think it's best for everyone to focus on his recovery."

"That's very generous of you, Andrea." Carol sipped her coffee. "Are you comfortable with that?"

"I think so, although something Sean's mother and father told us makes me really wonder if we should let this get swept under the carpet. My decisions and actions were never against Sean. They were for me and the children." Andrea reached for a cookie. "I shouldn't, but I can't resist."

She took a bite and chewed slowly. "I value all life, including Sean's. I don't know what happened to him to make him so violent, but I don't wish him any harm. I just want to keep the children and I safe from his violence. I hope he gets the treatment he needs and can have a better life, someday."

"Except it won't ever be with you or the children." Carol put a hand over one of Andrea's.

"That part is decided. Even his mother accepts that fact."

"You saw her? She's here?"

"We got together three times before they went back to Canada. And yes, she understands." Andrea took another bite of the cookie. "How about I take the plate to the kids and come back, so we won't be interrupted? There's more you need to know."

"Go."

Andrea came back and sat down. "Since coming out of the induced coma, Sean has been very agitated and unpredictable. He sent one orderly home with stitches and a nurse to emergency with a broken collar bone. He was sedated and in restraints during the medevac flight."

"This doesn't sound good."

"No, it doesn't. I'm just thankful he is nowhere near me or the children. But, his mother and father finally broke cover. Sean has a history of abusing, torturing and killing animals that goes back to when he was seven years old."

"Oh my God. Did they not report him?"

Andrea shook her head. "Lorna's always been very protective of Sean. Now I know why. I think she was trying to protect the family pride and honor."

"Misplaced on both accounts. Childhood abuse of animals is part of the profile of psychopathic murderers."

"I know. I spent several hours on the internet after they went back to Canada."

"Why did his parents keep it hidden? More importantly, why did they tell you now?"

"I think they both realize Sean has no more natural inhibitions. He's reacting raw. He's like a wild animal. If he feels the least bit threatened, he goes into fight mode. And fight to kill."

Carol sat back. "I can't imagine being married to someone like that. I'm amazed you lasted this long."

Andrea sighed. "Maybe now people will begin to understand why I left on the eve of his return. I was terrified of him before he left. I couldn't imagine seeing him when he got back after another six months in combat."

"So, what's next for you?"

"I'm going ahead with the divorce. And, I'm going to sell the house in New Jersey."

"Can you do that? Is the house in your name?" Carol topped up their coffee and sat down again.

"It's in my name, yes, but I also have full power of attorney."

Carol took another cookie and nibbled at it. "I'll do extra yoga later."

Andrea snaked out her hand and snagged another cookie. "I run after small children. I need sustenance. By the way," she said, "before I forget, I'm going up to New Jersey in a couple of weeks to get my Tricare file and card. I'll be able to put in a claim."

"I was pretty shocked at the bill. Thank goodness for medical plans!"

"I can't begin to imagine what Sean's plan will be covering. A year of trauma care and rehabilitation? He'll be a million dollar man sooner rather than later."

"All of it's covered, right?" Carol stood up and took their mugs to the dishwasher.

"Yes. He's on full pay; his medical bills are covered one hundred percent. And a portion of his pay will come into my account for child support. Standard practice." Andrea stood up. "The army takes care of its own, that's for sure. It'll also take care of the children."

"Well, it may take care of its own but what about spouses like you? What's being done about the abuse?"

"I know, Carol. But there are no perfect employers, and there are always imperfect employees. I want to believe they're just doing their best to handle the bad apples. Let's face it, the majority of employers don't require their employees to go into the line of fire as a condition of employment."

"I hear you, Andrea. You are a kind and empathetic soul, but I'm not sure if I could be that way in your shoes, given what you've gone through."

"I put those shoes on the day I accepted Sean's proposal. My sister-in-law asked me straight up *what happened to for better or for worse?* and I realize now, that part ended when I felt my children might grow up without their mother."

"You thought he would kill you if you left?"

"I still do." Andrea walked towards the solarium. "A year in rehabilitation is a long time. But, if and when he gets out, I don't believe we'll be safe anywhere. He may be brain injured but he remembers us, and he's obsessed. We're not out of the woods yet, by any means." Andrea shivered.

"You have a major support network here now." Carol stood up and took her mug to the sink. "By the time Sean gets out, he may have moved on emotionally."

"I hope so," Andrea said. "I doubt it, but I hope so."

Chapter Fifteen

THE SMELL OF ROTTING FOOD ASSAILED HER NOSE as she walked into the New Jersey house. It was a sharp contrast to the sweet smells from the flowers of late June blooming in gardens and patio pots up and down the street. She gagged on the smell and her eyes burned as she made her way towards the source. In the weeks since Sean's accident, no one had gone in. Louise was too busy with working, caring for her children, and visiting Richard. Andrea had spoken to Pam and Jim a few time about their totaled truck, but hadn't asked them to check the house.

I need help with this, she realized. *I can't do it all in one day alone.* She found her personal phone book, looked up Louise and Richard's neighbor and called.

"Pam, hi. I'm so glad you're home. It's Andrea." Andrea walked towards the kitchen and stopped. The smell was overpowering. "How are things going with the insurance? Did they replace the truck, finally?

"Oh, thank goodness. I was hoping there wouldn't be trouble over that." She walked into the living room, sat in her chair, and looked around. "Is there any chance you have a couple of hours to spare? I need to clean out the fridge, bring out the trash, and clean thoroughly. A real estate agent is coming late this afternoon.

"Yes, I'm selling. Sean won't need a place this big if and when he gets out of rehab." Andrea held up one hand and crossed her fingers—then smiled. "Thanks so much, Pam. I really appreciate it. If you bring some milk, I can make us some tea or coffee."

ANDREA WAS PUTTING OUT A LARGE GREEN TRASH BAG when Pam arrived with a picnic basket half an hour later. She pushed some stray hairs away from her face and breathed in the fresh air, a welcome relief from the reeking air inside.

"Thanks so much for coming. I'm getting the kitchen under control. All the windows are open, so it's starting to smell a bit better."

"I brought some leftovers we can munch on when we get hungry." Pam looked at Andrea closely. "Something is different. This is not the Andrea I talked to two months ago."

"Starting the divorce proceedings lifted a big weight from my soul." Andrea smiled. "I love my work. The kids are doing really well. I'm in a happy place, now."

"It also looks like you're in love. You're practically vibrating with happiness." Pam walked through to the kitchen with her basket and set it down. "I can only imagine what this place smelled like when you called. It's ripe even now."

"It sort of took my breath away," Andrea said.

Pam looked at her for a moment with a strained expression. "Andrea," she said, "there's something I want you to know. Jim and I had no idea about the abuse. Had we known, we would have tried to help you. I hope you believe that."

"I do believe you." Andrea picked up a sponge and started to clean the stove. "It happens more often than anyone is willing to admit. But, I have to take some responsibility for hiding it for so long."

"So, is it love, this new guy, I mean?"

Andrea's smile radiated the answer. "Yes. He's wonderful. He's kind, lovable, he has a great sense of humor, the kids love him, and he has a farm with lots of animals."

"Oh, God, this is just like being transferred to new base housing. Clean the house Mary Poppins' clean." Pam picked up a cloth, soaked it in the bucket of soap and water, squeezed it out and started washing down the cupboards. "Are you living with him?"

"Not yet. But, we're talking. His father has a new lady friend and may be moving in with her. She's trying to convince him. He's resisting, but not seriously."

"Any word on Sean's progress? It's been, what, almost three months, now?" Pam rinsed her cloth.

"He has severe memory problems. He doesn't remember whole periods of his life. For some reason, though, he remembers I left him. Apparently his blood pressure just soars if he's asked about me or the kids."

"Any talk of him being released?" Pam moved on to the counters.

"Not by a long shot. He has explosive tantrums. That's all I can call them, from what I've been told." Andrea looked in the oven. It was as clean as the day she'd left. "He'll be fine and then just erupt, for no reason anyone can pinpoint."

"That sounds a bit scary, given the martial arts training he's had."

"Exactly. It's what happened back in Massachusetts. He reacted to being physically touched and slammed a nurse against a wall. Broke her collarbone."

"Lucky he didn't kill her. Jim's had the same training and he's told me what he's capable of." Pam put down her cloth and looked at Andrea. "You're lucky to be alive, you know that."

Andrea looked at her and took a deep breath. "I know."

She walked into Pam's arms. They hugged silently for a long moment as tears streamed down Andrea's cheeks.

The real estate agent walked into the house and shook her head. "Did something die here?"

Andrea stifled a laugh. "You could say that. No one has lived here for almost three months. My ex-husband was in an accident and no one has come in for some time. I'm here to get it all cleaned up and deodorized."

"I hope you don't expect me to show it smelling like this?" The agent started to walk through the main level without touching anything.

Andrea's smile faded. "I live and work full-time in Massachusetts. I'm raising two small children, alone. My ex-husband is in a rehabilitation facility and is not capable of doing anything. If you want me to hire someone to fumigate, just say so.

"If you want this listing, you tell me what needs to be done and then you help me do it or I will find another listing agent."

The agent stopped and looked at Andrea. "I don't get paid enough to take a listing like this. Please, feel free to find another agent." She walked towards the door.

Andrea threw up her hands. "Okay, wait. I don't have time to find another agent. Please, help me here. I just want to sell this and get on with my life."

The woman looked at Andrea long and hard and finally relented. "Okay, I'm a mom, too. Tell you what, let me give you the name of a good fumigation company. Get them in and we'll go from there.

"We can work online and by phone. Take out what you need but leave enough that it looks like a family home. Know what I mean?"

Andrea breathed a sigh of relief. "Yes, I have a pretty good idea about how to stage the house. Thank you."

"I'm sorry, I dumped on you. As a mom, you know how it is. I'm sleep deprived. The little one has an ear infection. I'm up several times a night."

"Tell me about it." The two women smiled at each other as they went out onto the porch and into the fresh air.

"You left him?" The agent crooked her head towards Andrea.

"Yep. Abuse. I refused to take it."

"I'm getting a lot of those, these days. Our guys are coming back damaged. It's not pretty." She fell silent.

Andrea looked at the agent more closely. "You, too?"

"Yeah, me too." She walked quickly back to her car and drove away.

"I MISSED YOU GUYS!" ANDREA CUDDLED EMILY AND SIMON IN CLOSE as Kyle looked on. "Just a weekend away and I'm sure you both grew!

She looked up at Kyle and smiled. "You'd better not grow any more or I won't be able to reach up to kiss you!"

"Don't worry. I stopped growing a few years ago, except when I'm around you." He winked lasciviously as Andrea dissolved into laughter.

"Okay, I know when I'm beaten in the innuendo department. You win."

"How did it go with the listing agent?" Kyle bent down as Simon clambered onto his back.

"She was reluctant at first, but I won her over. She's a mom, too. I played the sympathy card big time. The fumigators are coming tomorrow."

"Oh, that bad?"

"Worse. The agent asked if someone had died."

"Ouch. That's bad." Kyle adjusted Simon on his back. "You'll stay here for the night?"

"Can't think of another place I'd rather stay." Andrea winked as she picked up Emily for a big hug. "How's my Peanut? Did you miss me?"

"Portia does tricks, Mommy. She can count!" Emily put her hands in Andrea's curls. "Your hair is so pretty, Mommy."

"Thank you, sweetie. Your hair is just as pretty. It's just like mine." Andrea smiled and nuzzled her nose into Emily's neck.

"That tickles!" Emily wriggled out of her mom's grasp and ran giggling to Kyle who swooped her up and did the same thing as Simon slithered off his back. The laughter and giggles continued as they all strolled outside in the late afternoon sunshine to bring apples to the horses.

Kyle's arm was wrapped around Andrea as they snuggled in his bed. "When are you going to move in with me? It's been three months. We're together almost every night. You know Emily and Simon love it here."

Andrea nestled her head on his chest and listened to the slow rhythmic beating of his heart. "And they adore you. I do want us all to live together. Guess it's time to make some plans.

"Will your dad mind sharing his house?" Andrea smiled. She already knew the answer.

"He's asked me to get you all here. Plus, I think he's getting ready to pop the big question to Janet."

"Really? He wants to marry her?" Andrea raised her head up in surprise.

"He's not the kind of man who could live in sin. He's pretty old-fashioned that way."

"But, he'll stay over at her place a whole weekend."

"That's different." Kyle grinned.

"Tell me how it's different," Andrea teased.

"He's just visiting for the weekend. It's not the same thing as living together." Kyle chuckled. "Sounds pretty lame, doesn't it?"

"Yes, it does." Andrea agreed. "But, I like the logic. If it works for them, it works for me."

They were interrupted by Simon calling out. "Sounds like a diaper change is in order. How's it going in the how-to pee-like-a-man department?"

"I think he's getting the idea watching me out behind the barn. But I read online that he's still too young to do it standing up. He needs to have some training pants and a child potty and do it sitting down for a few more months."

"Look who's becoming the potty training expert." Andrea laughed. "So, sitting first, standing later."

"Correct." Kyle chuckled. "How about I go see him and get him organized?"

"I'll get Emily up and dressed. Meet you in the kitchen in a few minutes. I can smell the coffee."

"ROSIE AND I WILL BE CHECKING THE FENCE LINES THIS MORNING. I should be back late morning. Will you still be here?" Kyle lifted Simon out of his high chair, set him on the floor and cleaned toast crumbs off the tray.

"Yes. Val told me to take the day off after she heard about the weekend cleaning binge in New Jersey. I really love working for that woman." Andrea wiped the counter and hung the tea towel to dry. "We'll hang out with Portia and your dad for a while and then make everyone lunch."

"Sounds great!" Kyle opened his arms to Andrea and gave her a warm hug. "See you for lunch."

Andrea watched Kyle and Rosie set off towards the upper pasture and smiled. *This is my life now.*

ANDREA WAS WATCHING EMILY PUT PORTIA THROUGH SOME OF HER PACES when she heard Rosie barking. Looking up the hill, she saw the dog running at full speed towards them, alone. *Oh my God. Where is Kyle?*

"Tom! Something's wrong. Rosie's coming back alone. Watch Emily and Simon." Andrea ran back to the house for her phone and the paper with Rosie's commands. She took precious seconds to grab a water bottle and her work gloves before running out to the pasture gate with Rosie leading the way. *God, please don't let him be hurt.*

"Rosie. Find Kyle." Andrea commanded and ran after the dog, which shot up the hill towards the eastern fence line. Running after small children had given Andrea regular workouts but Rosie was too fast. "Rosie. Steady."

The dog slowed, looked back and then waited until Andrea had almost caught up before resuming her search. Andrea followed Rosie and was relieved to see Kyle huddled over a lamb that was stuck in a pile of old fencing. The ewe hovered nearby.

Andrea stopped, put her hands on her knees and bent over to catch her breath. "Thank God, you're okay," she said, in between dragging air into her heaving lungs. "What's up?"

"Hey, Rosie. Good girl." The dog lay down, panting. "Have you got your phone with you?"

"Yes."

"Good. Call down to my dad and ask him to bring some bolt cutters. I can't get this little guy out and he's already pretty badly cut. I don't want to leave him. He's frantic and will just injure himself worse."

"You go. Your dad is watching over Emily and Simon. I'll take over until you get back." Andrea pulled on her work gloves after taking a long pull from the water bottle.

"Okay. Rosie, hold." Kyle stood up as Andrea crouched down and cradled the struggling lamb. "She'll keep the ewe from interfering. I'll be back in a few minutes."

Andrea spoke quietly to the lamb and held it carefully to relieve the pressure on its neck. The lamb bleated in pain and fear. Andrea noticed the ewe moving towards her and was relieved when Rosie moved in between her and the anxious mother. The ewe backed away to a safer distance. Rosie wouldn't let her closer.

As she held the squirming animal, Andrea kept talking softly to it. The lamb gradually quieted as she spoke. "Good boy. You'll be fine. You're in good hands. You'll be out and running around soon. Shhh. That's it."

Moments later, the sound of an ATV broke the quiet as Kyle raced the machine up to them. The lamb wriggled at the sound of the machine but Andrea spoke quietly in its ear and cradled it.

"All right. Let's get this little one out and see what's up." Kyle cut the engine, brought out the bolt cutters and within a minute the lamb was freed into Andrea's arms.

She kneaded the neck area and checked the cuts. "He looks fine. None of the cuts is deep. He won't need stitches. I think we can let his mother take over from here. She'll clean him up. He'll be easy to pick out from the other lambs. That wire is pretty rusty. I'll check with Val if it's too early for his first tetanus shot."

Andrea set the lamb down, watched it run straight to its mother, and smiled. "That little drama is over." She stood up and stretched, taking off her gloves. "What's next?"

"Well, my dad has the kids. Apart from Rosie and the sheep, we're up here alone. It's a beautiful sunny warm morning." Kyle put his arm up and scratched his head. "Are you busy for the next half hour or so?"

Andrea grinned. "Did you bring any protection with you?"

"No." Kyle's grin faded.

"I did." Andrea grinned and dangled the little packet in front of him. "I carry it with me all the time when I'm around you."

"I always knew you were special." Kyle unbuckled his coveralls and let them fall to his waist. "If you come over here, I can show you just how special."

"I LOVE MY WORK BUT I DON'T LOVE ALL THE ACHES AND PAINS THAT COME WITH IT." Val stretched and arched her shoulders. "You got any plans for the Fourth of July weekend?"

"Well, I was thinking about moving the children and me in with Kyle."

Val stopped stretching. "Did I hear you right? You're going to shack up with Kyle full-time? Tom okay with this?"

"It was partly his idea." Andrea grinned. "Apparently Tom is going to pop the question to Janet. Make an honest woman out of her."

Val's eyes widened. "Ooh! I think I just heard the juiciest piece of gossip in the entire county. Tell me more. I have book club tonight."

Andrea laughed. "But, you can't say anything, silly. Janet will be there."

"So?" Andrea packed up her kit bag.

"You don't want to spoil his surprise do you?"

"Hmph. Maybe not." Val snorted. "Damn. This is the best piece of news around here in a long time. You moving in with Kyle is also great news. I knew you two were meant to be together. Just had a feeling."

"I had it too, very early on. It felt so right." Andrea hesitated. "Can I tell you something? You have to promise never to tell anyone."

Val's gossip radar was tucked away. "By the look on your face, it must be important. I won't say anything. Can I tell Casey though?"

"Yes. But only him." Andrea drew in a deep breath and let it out slowly. "When Sean's mother was here in April, she told me Sean started torturing and killing animals when he was seven years old. As he got older, he kept journals. Called them science experiments."

Val looked at her in horror. "Oh God, Andrea. And you had no idea."

"None." Andrea felt hot tears welling up and blinked them back. "I keep reminding myself that I have two wonderful children."

Val laid a hand on her shoulder. "Keep remembering that, Andrea. What a horrible thing to learn about your ex-husband. You must be devastated."

"I am. I've barely told anyone. Kyle knows; he was there when she broke cover. Carol knows." Andrea wiped a hand across her eyes. "It's giving me nightmares. Thank goodness for Kyle."

"How did his cruelty and violence tendencies get through the military screenings?"

"I have no idea. From what I've found out, unless he had a history of social or psychiatric problems going in, they'd be happy to have him." Andrea shook her head. "He has above average intelligence, has a college degree and he's always been athletic and into martial arts. He was an ideal candidate."

The two women walked towards their vehicles. "This is so totally against everything I value and believe in. I don't think I will ever see him again. Whatever sympathy I may have had for Sean is well and truly gone now."

Andrea stood beside Val's old van. "Moving in with Kyle will be the start of a new chapter in my life. I'm ready for it."

The two women hugged in silence.

JANET WIPED HER HANDS ON A TOWEL and watched as Tom's pickup turned up her driveway. She noticed how clean his truck was. *It's not even Sunday,* she mused. *Wonder what he's up to?*

She waited as he parked and got out. *He's all dressed up for a weekday. And he's carrying a bunch of flowers! What's this all about?*

"Tom. Good to see you. You're a bit early. Dinner won't be ready for another half hour." She stood aside to let him into the mud room off the kitchen.

Tom stood awkwardly, his height filling the small ante room. He stuck out the arm with the flowers. "Thought these would look pretty on your sideboard."

Janet smiled. "They would indeed. Thank you so much for buying them. Come on in. Maybe you'd like a beer?"

"Yes, a beer would be great." He followed her into the sparkling kitchen that smelled of roast beef. "We having a roast tonight?"

"Yes. It'll give me leftovers for another dinner and a couple of lunch sandwiches for Emily, Simon and I. I have a busy week with several orders for the Sweet Repose." She took the flowers and went into her dining room to find a vase. "Beer's in the fridge."

Tom walked over to the fridge, pulled out a beer and opened it. He took a long thirsty pull on the frosty brew and sat down at the kitchen table.

Janet returned with a tall vase and headed for the sink. "I'll just get these in some water. They're lovely, Tom. Thank you."

Tom had another sip of his beer.

Janet took a pair of clippers out of a drawer and opened up the brightly colored cellophane. As she peeled the plastic wrap back, an envelope fell on the counter. "Oh good, they put in some cut flower food."

She put some water in the vase and then picked up her scissors and snipped the end off the envelope. She shook it over the water but nothing came out. She snipped back some more and shook it over the water again.

"There's something hard in here."

Tom started to grin.

Janet snipped the top off the envelope, peered inside and gasped.

"Thomas Sheridan. You rogue! What is this?" Janet shook out a ring into the palm of her hand. She turned to look at him, her eyes shining. "Is this your idea of a marriage proposal?"

"Time to make an honest woman out of you." Tom stood up and opened his arms to her. "Figured you'd want a ring. Most women do."

"Before you put this ring on me, I want you to ask me properly." She smiled up at him and handed him the ring.

Tom held the modest solitaire diamond in his large, work-worn hands. "Janet Henderson, will you do me the honor of becoming Mrs. Sheridan at your earliest opportunity?" He coughed. "Please?"

Janet laughed. "Oh Tom, you know I will. We'll do it right here. Nothing fancy. How do you define earliest opportunity?"

"Before the end of summer?"

"I'm sure I can manage that." Janet watched as he slipped the ring onto her finger. "In the meantime, you can start moving in your things."

"You want us to live here?"

"I need my kitchen. Besides, there's a few things need fixing around here. I expect you to do your share of the work around here. Not like at your place." Janet tried to look stern but her eyes were sparkling. "You need to remember how things work when there's a woman in charge."

"Seems I do." Tom smiled down at her. "It's been a long time, but I'm sure it will come back quickly."

"I'll be here to guide you, my dear." Janet reached up a hand and caressed his cheek. "Let's get to work on dinner and see what happens next."

Chapter Sixteen

ANDREA STRETCHED AND LET HER ARM DROP OVER KYLE'S CHEST. She stroked her hand through his mass of fine blonde hair. "Wake up, big guy. Your dad's getting married today."

Kyle's eyes opened slowly. "What time is it? Is it even light yet?"

Andrea chuckled. "Some farm boy you are. It's light enough for you to get out to the barn while I get the kids up." She threw the covers off both of them and dove off the bed before Kyle could grab her.

"C'mon. Coffee's ready. We need to be out of here in less than three hours." She pulled on her robe and padded out of the room after opening the curtains and pulling up the blinds. There was a slight glow on the eastern horizon. Birds were already singing in the dim light as Andrea made her way down to the kitchen.

She turned on lights and nodded in sleepy satisfaction at the tidy pile in the corner near the door. An electric cooler full of salads was humming. A gaily wrapped gift box sat beside it. Their shoes were all clean and lined up at the door. A bag of toys sat nearby.

She was pouring two coffees when Kyle came down the stairs in a t-shirt and boxers. "I put clean coveralls in the mud room. Meet you back here in an hour for breakfast? Then we'll take turns watching the kids and having showers."

"Sounds good. Coffee's great. Thanks. See you later." Kyle took his mug off to the barn as the first rays of the sun peeked over the horizon.

Andrea sat at the table and looked around. Outside, she could see her gleaming new van waiting to transport them to the wedding. She'd bought it with some of the money from the sale of the house in New Jersey. The rest was banked to be shared with Sean when the divorce was finalized.

She sipped on her coffee and smiled. *Laskin is my home now. It feels like I've lived here for years and not just four months.* She thought about calling Carol, knowing she'd be up, but decided against it. They were both getting their animals ready before leaving for the big day.

"SO, WHEN ARE YOU AND KYLE GOING TO MAKE IT OFFICIAL?" Carol and Andrea stood together, looking on as Kyle made his way to stand in front of the flower bed that formed the backdrop for the ceremony. A white arbor had been placed in front of the steps leading up to the verandah of Janet's home. It was festooned with red and pink carnations.

"My divorce should be final before Christmas. We're thinking of getting married Christmas day if we can talk Reverend Chilcott into it." Andrea smiled as Kyle saw her and gave a little wave.

"I'm sure he'd be happy to do it. He's very fond of you both." Carol reached down and took Emily's hand as she came running over. "Hi, Peanut. What a pretty dress you have on today."

"I get to hold Gamma's flowers when she gets married." Emily vibrated up and down on her toes.

"Looks like you're pretty excited." Carol laughed and looked over at Andrea. "I didn't have a pretty little girl to hold my flowers when I married Devin."

There was a definite change in the buzz of conversation as the reverend came out of the house with Tom. Both men took their place near Kyle as people broke from groups and found their seats. A flutist, who had been wandering among the guests, moved in behind the arbor. Once out of sight, the ethereal music seemed to float over the gathering.

Then a hush fell over the guests, as Janet emerged through her front door wearing a simple cream-colored dress and bolero jacket. She carried a small bouquet of red roses. She smiled as she made her way down the steps to stand beside Tom.

Kyle and Devin stood together watching as people began laying claim to spots at the tables that had been set up.

"I'm so happy to see both Tom and Janet finding happiness

again. They both deserve it." Devin shook Kyle's hand as the two men clinked beer bottles in congratulations to the newlyweds. "You did a good job up there."

Kyle laughed and took a sip of his beer. "Wasn't much for me to do. Just stand there and give my dad away."

"He looks like the happiest man here, today."

"He sure does. I never would have believed this possible just a few months ago." Kyle waved to a guest. "Since Andrea and Janet came into our lives, we've changed. For the better, of course."

ANDREA AND CAROL WALKED INTO JANET'S BUSTLING KITCHEN, where six women were busy setting out platters of cold chicken, salads, rolls and condiments. A dozen dessert trays sat on one end of the long counter.

"Everything under control in here?"

"It's all under control. But you can take some plates out to the buffet, if you would." Val was in charge. "Where are Emily and Simon? I thought they'd be glued to you with all these strangers around."

Andrea laughed. "Flynn and Gregory are making sure they stay out of trouble. They'll be taken home in an hour or so."

"When do my book club ladies get to cater your wedding?" Val handed off a platter of fried chicken.

"We're going to have a small, private ceremony on Christmas Eve."

"It may be private, but I expect an invitation."

"Even if it's Christmas Eve?"

"Especially if it's Christmas Eve." Val chortled. "Reverend Chilcott thinks you walk on water after you cured his dog of yapping at everyone he sees. I think you're probably the only person in the county he would agree to marry off on Christmas Eve."

Andrea was smiling as she left the busy kitchen. She greeted people and gradually worked her way towards the buffet with the platter she was carrying.

"Can I help you with that?" Kyle had made his way over to join her. "I don't know about you, but I'm hungry."

"I'm famished. We didn't really eat any lunch, and breakfast was hours ago." Andrea set down the platter and got two plates and some cutlery for them. "Emily and Simon should be around here somewhere. They need to eat, too."

"They'll be fine. Flynn will make sure they're taken care of. Let's you and I fill our plates and go sit down somewhere in the shade."

Taking their plates of food, they found a couple of chairs that had been set up under a sprawling oak. "Too bad Richard, Louise, and the children couldn't be here, today."

"Richard's still not cleared to drive very far. And still gets vertigo." Andrea swatted away a persistent fly. "He should be fine to travel by Christmas though. I know Louise really wants to bring them all here and spend Christmas together, especially if we're tying the knot."

"What about Sean's parents?"

"They won't come. It's too far for them." Andrea speared up some potato salad. "They never came before, so I don't expect that to change."

"Did they ever tell anyone about Sean's childhood problems?"

"Not that I know of. I'm sure Lorna would have said something during one of my calls to update her on the kids."

Kyle shook his head. "Someone needs to know. He's a loaded gun waiting to go off."

"Let's not talk about him anymore. It's too nice a day." Andrea patted his knee. "He's far away from us."

Kyle munched on fried chicken and potato salad and pointed out Emily and Simon, who were now sitting with plates of food next to Janet, Tom and Gregory, as Flynn hovered over them all.

"My father adores them. When I look at him now, I remember him the way he used to be with me at Emily's age. His joy at watching a child grow and learn has come back." Kyle looked over at Andrea. "Think we could manage with one more?"

"At least one more and maybe two if I can do it full-time."

"What will Val say?"

"She'd be first in line to congratulate us. She's already demanded an invite to whatever wedding we plan. Especially if it's Christmas Eve."

"How about we plan for Christmas and keep practicing in the meantime?" Kyle raised his eyebrows suggestively.

Andrea laughed. "That sounds like a fine idea." Setting down their empty plates, they held hands and watched Tom entertaining his grandchildren.

IT WAS STILL A BIT LIGHT WHEN ANDREA AND KYLE GOT BACK TO THE FARM. They looked in on Emily and then checked on Simon. Both were sound asleep. They said goodbye to Flynn and Gregory and began turning off lights.

"I don't know about you, but I'm going to be ready for bed pretty soon. That was a long day."

"But what a lovely day. I hope our wedding will be just as special."

"If you're there, it's guaranteed to be special." Kyle took her hand and walked her towards the stairs. "Let's sit downstairs for a little while and have some private, quiet time. What do you say?"

Andrea stifled a yawn. "A few minutes, sure. Want a cup of tea?"

"I'll put the kettle on."

They had just sat down with their steaming mugs of tea when they heard a scratching sound at the mud room door. Kyle walked over and opened it.

"Rosie! What's up, girl?" He looked on in astonishment as Rosie ran into the kitchen and pulled at Andrea's pant leg. "This is new. She's never done that to me or anyone else. She's never even been in the house since she was a puppy. This is bizarre."

Andrea put her mug down and stood up. "It's Bonnie. It's her time. Rosie, let's go."

Kyle shook his head and followed Rosie and Andrea to the dark barn.

"EVERYTHING SEEMS TO BE PERFECTLY NORMAL. She'll probably drop the foal in the next hour or two." Andrea patted Bonnie's heaving flank and felt another powerful contraction. "If it weren't the middle of the night, I'd get Emily up to see this. But it will be quite a surprise for them in the morning."

Kyle paced outside the stall. "Are you sure she's all right?"

"Yes, she's fine. The foal is in place. We should see legs soon, judging by those contractions."

"I've seen more animals born than I can count but with Bonnie, it feels different. She's more like family than a farm animal."

Andrea smiled in the soft light. "She's doing fine, Kyle. Her foal will be standing up on its own within a few minutes, I'd say. Our baby will need a few more months."

Rosie lay down and watched Bonnie without making a sound. She'd seen the lambs being born each year. This wasn't new, just a bit different.

Kyle wasn't so sure. "This is Bonnie's first. Shouldn't we call Val and get her over here, in case?"

Andrea chuckled. "I can see you're going to be so relaxed when it's time to deliver our baby."

"What do you mean, *when it's time*? You're not pregnant are you?" Kyle stopped pacing and turned to look at her.

Andrea smiled at the look on his face. "Well, I'm three weeks late now. Chances are..."

Kyle's eyes widened even as a bright smile suffused his face. "Are you serious?"

She laughed. "You sound like me! But yes, chances are we're pregnant. You okay with that?"

"You know I am." Kyle dodged around Bonnie and curled Andrea into a warm embrace. "You know I want you to have our child. I so hope you're pregnant."

"We'll know for sure tomorrow. The kit says I am. But, I stopped by the doctor's on Thursday and will have the official results on Monday. She's confident I am. Oh! Here come the legs! Stand back."

Bonnie gave a push as Andrea got a firm grip on the forelegs and pulled. The colt emerged in its sac as Bonnie looked back. Andrea pulled the foal towards its mother who was already licking it and nudging it, as if to check that all was in order.

"Look at that." Kyle watched as Bonnie nuzzled her foal and licked it over. "She's a real motherly type."

"They're bonding already." Andrea stood up and let Bonnie take over. "She'll make a wonderful mom, that's obvious."

The mare kept licking and nuzzling the foal and gently whinnied and snickered to it.

"Look, she's already trying to stand up!" Andrea watched in wonder as the foal, just minutes old, tried to stand up. She fell over a couple of times but Bonnie kept licking her and encouraging her. The foal finally stood on four rickety legs as Bonnie continued her ministrations.

"Do you believe this?" Kyle stared on in wonder, running a hand over his head. "My first foal. My first Canadian horse. This is beyond special."

Andrea smiled and yawned. "How about we all get some sleep? I think Bonnie has everything under control. We don't have many hours before Emily and Simon will need us."

"But, what about her name? Shouldn't we name her?"

"Tomorrow. I need some sleep." Andrea yawned again and started to walk away.

Kyle looked at the foal for a moment longer and then followed Andrea to bed.

"EMILY. SIMON. WE HAVE A LITTLE SURPRISE FOR YOU." Andrea finished putting away their breakfast dishes and grinned at them. "Let's get you both ready to go to the barn. We have something to show you."

It wasn't long before Andrea and the children were walking into the morning coolness of the old barn. Kyle had been there for over an hour. Andrea smiled when she spotted him petting the newborn foal, which now stood on more sturdy legs. "Couldn't stay away?"

Kyle grinned sheepishly. "I did manage to get my chores done first. I'm just taking a break."

Andrea chuckled. "Guess we'll all be taking a lot of breaks today. Come and see, Emily. It's a foal – a baby horse. She was just born last night."

Kyle picked up Simon so he could see into the stall. Andrea picked Emily up.

"Oh, Mommy. A real baby horse. What's her name?" Emily reached out to touch the soft muzzle of the now-curious foal.

"Well, we thought you could help us name her." Andrea glanced over to Kyle, who nodded with a smile. "What's your absolute most favorite name, Emily?"

"Ariel! The Little Mermaid. Let's call her Ariel. Please, Mommy?"

Kyle looked confused. "I really like the name but what's The Little Mermaid?"

Andrea laughed. "Can't imagine how you could have missed The Little Mermaid. The movie came out in 1989."

"Have you seen any theaters around Laskin?" Kyle chuckled as the foal tried to chew the sleeve of Emily's jacket. "I don't think I went to a movie theater until I was twelve years old. And it wasn't to see The Little Mermaid."

"I guess not. Not at that manly age." Andrea held on to Emily as Bonnie came over to get some attention and the apple that Andrea was offering. The foal abandoned Emily's sleeve and set to busily nursing.

"Ariel it is, then. Welcome to the Sheridan family, Ariel." Kyle put an arm around Andrea as he held on to Simon. "Welcome to our family."

CHAPTER SEVENTEEN
NOVEMBER 2011

THE PRESIDING PANEL MEMBER looked around at her colleagues. "We're all in agreement, then? Let the record show unanimous agreement among the panel members.

"Sean Garrett is hereby released from the United States Army on medical grounds. Let the record show we have assessed his disability at eighty percent. Let the record further show that, due to chronic traumatic brain injuries that he sustained prior to his service, while in service and in a subsequent vehicle accident while on authorized leave, he is ineligible for any further military duty. We sincerely thank him for his service to his country."

ANDREA RECEIVED A REGISTERED LETTER and immediately called his parents.

Andrea read the decision to Lorna.

"Do you have any idea what this means?"

"What it means is that Sean will be covered by disability payments and the children will have financial support until they're twenty-six. It looks like he may get out though. That's what worries me. With his unpredictable temper he'll never function normally. Can he stay with you?"

"He can't possibly come here. Fred's developed a heart condition. He couldn't take the stress of Sean's unpredictable behavior. It would kill him."

"Well, the Army is supposed to take care of its own. It's time it stepped up to the plate with Sean. I want nothing to do with him."

Andrea set her phone down just as baby Andre announced another imminent need to nurse.

SEAN PULLED UP IN FRONT OF RICHARD AND LOUISE'S BROWNSTONE ON A WARM SPRING DAY. He'd been in rehab for almost two years. He was driving a weekend rental with his tote bag in the back. He didn't know where else to go. He'd gone by his old home and had seen another family there. Two small children. He almost thought they were his until he realized Emily was now eight years old and Simon was almost seven.

He looked around, still unsure what to do. Down the street, some kids were skateboarding. A few people were out doing spring clean-up. A child's tricycle lay on its side on a lawn. Clouds were gathering that would soon drop a spring shower on everyone and everything. He walked up to the door and rang the bell as a rumble of distant thunder rolled through the air.

Louise opened the door. "Sean? Is that you? Come in." She called back into the house. "Richard, come here. It's Sean!"

Richard came to the door, looked at Sean and nodded his head. "Hey, man. Finally got out? C'mon on in before it rains."

Sean looked at them both. "Can I stay here tonight? I have nowhere else to go."

"Sure, man. You're still family." They all went into the house as Richard closed the door. A pelting rain started to fall as a bolt of lightning sliced through the late afternoon sky.

Sean looked around the living room in a daze. "It seems different from the last time I was here."

Louise crossed her arms and looked at him without smiling. "I've made some changes. Bought some new furniture."

Richard pointed Sean to a chair and then sat down himself. "What are your plans, Sean?"

"I have none. I want to see my kids. Where are they?"

Richard looked down and shook his head. "You know I can't tell you that. It's in the court order that you are to have no further contact with Andrea or the children."

Sean looked at him with pleading eyes. "I haven't seen them for five years. I've thought of them every day. I need to see them. I need to hug and hold them. They're my kids." He put his head in his hands. "I went through hell in rehab. Thinking about them was the only way I got through it."

Richard went over and put a hand on his shoulder. Sean flinched and shied away. Stepping back quickly, Richard said, "Sorry, forgot. Don't touch." He could see that Sean was wound tight.

"Listen, they're doing great. Emily is in grade four now and sings like an angel. Simon is in grade one and can already read two grades ahead."

"Why can't I see them?" Sean looked up, his eyes misted with tears.

"You got violent, man. Way too violent." Richard looked away from Sean's direct gaze.

"I would never hurt my children, you know that."

Richard heard the flatness in Sean's voice. *Just defenseless women,* he thought. "I'm sure you wouldn't."

"Tell me where they are. I just want to see Emily and Simon one more time and then I'll move on, I promise."

"Can't do it, man." Richard looked at Louise, who shook her head and walked into the kitchen. "Stay for dinner and for the night. The kids can bunk in together, no problem. Can I get you anything?"

"I wouldn't say no to a beer."

"None in the house, sorry. How about a coffee?"

"Sure, thanks." Sean waited, his eyes on the iPhone on the table near Richard.

Richard went into the kitchen to get the coffee and didn't see Sean's triumphant look. When he returned, he didn't notice that his phone had been moved. He also didn't register that Sean was no longer asking how to contact Andrea.

"GOOD AFTERNOON, SIR. CAN I HELP YOU WITH SOMETHING?" The gun store clerk eyed the man cruising the store. "We have a special on Beretta handguns, today. You looking for anything in particular?"

Sean sized up the clerk. *What a jerkface. What you don't know about guns, pal, would fill a fucking book.*

"I'm looking for a used M16. You have any?"

The clerk suddenly straightened up. "Yes, sir. We have two in stock. Both used. Would you like to see them?"

Sean rolled his eyes. "If I asked you if you had some, don't you think I'd like to see them?"

The clerk paled at his hard look, nodded and scooted over to a door with three deadbolt locks. "Yes sir. Please follow me. They're in a special cabinet in the back."

Sean followed the clerk. He was wearing dark leather gloves and a brimmed hat. He'd seen the security cameras and kept his head down. He slouched, making himself appear shorter and stouter.

He noted with approval that the small room housing the high-powered guns had no security camera. *Unbelievable. Front door security camera and nothing in the back.*

The clerk drew out the first assault rifle and handed it to Sean. "It fires three-round bursts on semi-automatic. It has a 1-7 twist to shoot the heavier bullets needed at six hundred and a thousand yards."

"I know exactly what it does. I'm a competition marksman."

The clerk coughed. "As you know, then, this is very popular in High Power competition."

Sean sighted the gun, felt its heft. "I'll need a twenty round magazine and two, hundred-round boxes and directions to the nearest shooting range."

"Yes, sir." The nervous clerk left the room as Sean brought the gun out. "Ammunition is over here."

Sean showed the clerk his firearms identification card and paid in cash. He absently wondered whether he should just kill him. *No, not this one. This asshole is not my quarry.*

"Thank you for your patronage, sir." The clerk carefully put the gun in its case and bagged the ammunition. "If you have any questions, please call."

"Thanks." Sean picked up the gun case and left the store.

See you soon, Andrea. We're not finished.

Chapter Eighteen

Andrea looked around her spotless kitchen with weary satisfaction. Andre was teething and she was exhausted. She grabbed for the ringing phone before it could wake him from a much-needed afternoon nap.

"Hello?"

"Andrea, how long has it been?"

Andrea felt her throat constrict even as her entire body began to shake uncontrollably. She put her knuckles over her mouth in shock. "Sean? How did you get this number?"

"Some smart phones aren't so smart. Richard's, for one. It was so easy to get your name, address and phone. It was all there under A for Andrea."

Andrea frantically looked out the window, willing Kyle to come back. He was in the paddock with the horses. Ariel was in training with the saddle and a sack of grain on her back.

Sean sneered into the phone. "Your husband is looking very well these days. That plaid jacket he's wearing has seen better days, though. What's his name? I'd like to know who I'm going to kill today. I never knew their names all the other times."

Andrea was now pacing, pushing a hand through her hair, trying to figure out what to do. She spied Kyle's iPhone on the side table and clutched her heart in relief that, yet again, he'd forgotten to bring it with him. He still wasn't used to having one.

"Sean. I don't know what you're up to but don't do anything you'll be sorry for, please." As she cradled the house phone to her ear, she opened Kyle's phone and sent a text to Val to get the troopers out with no sirens, knowing she'd get it immediately. It was lambing season.

"Oh, I won't be sorry. I've been waiting years for this. I won't be sorry at all. Once I take care of you and your fucking farmer, Emily and Simon will be mine."

179

"They don't know you, Sean." Andrea looked at the clock, praying there were officers nearby.

"Here's what I want you to do, Andrea. You go on out and join your fucking farmer in the paddock. Go, kiss him goodbye."

Andrea steeled herself to stay calm. He could see Kyle. It meant he was hiding somewhere in the tree line. *Think. Think. Think.*

She walked to the mud room door and opened it. Stepping out into the frosty spring air, she called out to Kyle and waved the phone, "It's for you."

She heard Sean's raspy voice. "That wasn't smart, Andrea. I can pick him off any time I choose."

"I can't leave the baby, Sean. I have two more children now. If you want to pick us off, remember that. You'll have to kill me first before I let you get anywhere near my babies."

Andrea breathed a small sigh of relief when she saw Rosie trotting along with Kyle. As they got closer, Andrea mouthed 'Sean' and pointed to the phone. She made a small hand movement to warn him not to say anything to alert Sean that he was aware and crooked her chin to point up the hill.

Kyle nodded slightly and bent down, as if to tie up his boot. He whispered to Rosie, who immediately ran towards the pasture and began herding the sheep together. Kyle's boots crunched on the frosty gravel. When he reached Andrea, he winked at her and took the phone.

"Kyle, here."

"Kyle. So that's your name."

"Who is this?" Kyle pushed Andrea into the mud room and followed her. They closed the door and locked it.

"Why it's Sean Garrett. Your bitch's badass husband."

"She divorced you, Sean. I'm her badass husband now." Kyle nodded at Andrea, who was now speaking on his mobile with the state trooper detachment. She nodded back at him. The police were on their way.

"Tell you what, Sean. Why don't you come by the house and have a beer with me? You haven't seen Emily and Simon for a long time. We can get you all caught up and show you pictures."

Andrea's eyes widened as she shook her head wildly, pointing to the sleeping baby. *No! No! No!*

Kyle held up his hand and pointed out to the pasture, where Rosie had gathered the entire herd of sheep and was holding them in place. He nodded at her and mouthed the words 'I have a plan'.

"What do you say, man? Come, have a beer."

They both watched in surprise as a solitary figure in camouflage gear walked out of the trees and strode slowly down into the pasture. Andrea shuddered when she saw the rifle slung over Sean's shoulder and the ammo pouches at his waist. She watched him make his way toward them and noticed that he walked like an old man. Gone was the confident, strong gait of a young soldier.

Kyle stepped out into the yard and made his way towards the pasture gate. The chilly breeze held no warmth as he walked. The horses came over to the paddock fence and whinnied, but he ignored them. He was focused on the man coming down the hill. The man who wanted to kill him and his family. The man he had to stop, one way or another.

Andrea watched Kyle from the kitchen window. When Kyle's iPhone buzzed on the table she almost jumped out of her skin. She let Val's call go to message, picked up the phone and put it in her pants pocket and resumed her vigil at the window.

As Sean got closer, Kyle surveyed the scene. Rosie had the sheep in a loose group, making it appear that she was just keeping an eye on things, just as he had commanded. Sean was holding his weapon in a way that would allow him to swing it up and fire in a split second. Kyle only vaguely recognized the rifle from movies and news coverage of Iran and Iraq. He couldn't tell whether there was a safety and whether it was on or off.

He watched and waited until Sean was about ten yards away.

"Last time I saw you, you were in a hospital bed. You look pretty healthy now." Kyle saw Rosie's ears perk up at the sound of his voice. She was on high alert and waiting for a command. She was working the sheep. She completely ignored Sean.

"Where's Andrea? I want her to come out, now."

Kyle saw the hard gleam in Sean's eyes and knew he wasn't interested in casual conversation. "She's watching my son."

"I don't give a good goddamn if she's giving birth. I want her out here. Now."

Kyle watched as Sean fingered the gun stock. He called back to the house. "Andrea, come out here. Sean wants to talk to you."

Andrea heard Kyle's words and looked at her sleeping son. "Oh baby, I don't have a choice. I have to go out to them." She walked over and laid a hand on his downy head and leaned down to kiss his smooth brow.

With a heavy heart, she stepped outside and shivered in the cool afternoon breeze. She looked skyward at the scudding grey clouds that hid the sun. She saw a solitary eagle flying in wide circles overhead, its keening cry slicing through the air.

The gravel hurt her feet as she walked towards Kyle wearing only her soft house slippers. When he turned to look at her, she was grateful for the love in his eyes and prayed that they would survive this day

"Sean," she said, as she joined Kyle. "Why are you doing this? You have to know it's wrong. You'll be in lock-down for the rest of your life. You know that, don't you?"

"Don't you think I'm in a fucking prison already, Andrea?" Sean stopped just yards away from them on less than steady legs. "I can't remember things. My head hurts constantly. After I kill you, I'm going to see Emily and Simon one last time and then kill myself. I can't live like this. I don't have a life."

They both saw Sean's fingers moving toward the rifle trigger. Kyle whistled a command to Rosie. In an instant, she had the herd of sheep running in tight formation straight towards Sean. Sean looked confused; he turned at the noise. He appeared to stagger slightly and clumsily raised his rifle to aim just as the lead animals rushed into him. Sean reeled and went down, and Kyle saw the rifle slip from his grip.

Over the rumble of the shuffling, nervous sheep, he yelled, "Rosie, fetch!"

Rosie ran in amongst the bleating animals, which scattered in all directions, grabbed the rifle sling, and dragged it towards Kyle at full speed. Sean swore and struggled to get up as the agitated sheep milled around him. Kyle sprinted towards the dog and grabbed the rifle just as Sean stood up. "Rosie, that'll do."

The dog quickly came to stand by Kyle. Two state trooper cars sped up the pot-holed lane and roared into the pasture.

Andrea looked on wordlessly and sighed. *The warrior has finally fallen,* she shook her head. *His war is over. And so, thank God, is mine.*

"It's over, Sean." Kyle cradled the rifle as the officers pulled their squad cars into the pasture on either side of Sean and came out with their guns drawn. "You won't be killing anyone today."

Kyle handed the rifle to an officer and gathered Andrea into his arms.

"Sir, are you aware that this gun was set for automatic fire?" The officer looked at them both. "You wouldn't have stood a chance if he'd started firing."

Kyle and Andrea looked at each other and then the officer. Kyle spoke. "I decided this morning that this isn't a good day to die. Guess God heard me."

"How did Rosie know to fetch the rifle?" Andrea leaned against Kyle and willed her heart to beat normally as the officer went back to his cruiser with the loaded rifle that was now on safety.

"Dad and I taught her. When we were working around the property, I'd sometimes need a tool that my dad was using. We trained Rosie to fetch all kinds of stuff. It kept her busy and working." Kyle rubbed Andrea's back as the troopers cuffed Sean and deposited him in the back of one of the cruisers.

Kyle went over to give his report to an officer, with Rosie close on his heels. Andrea let her gaze roam over the now quiet pasture. Her turn would come, but for a few moments, she needed to let her adrenaline settle. The sheep had wandered back up to the higher pasture and were grazing peacefully. Several barn swallows were swooping through the air in a spring mating ritual. Apart from the police cars, there was no sign of the tense drama that had just taken place.

"Rosie sure saved this day." Andrea took Kyle's hand as he came back to her. "Guess it's my turn." Andrea pressed a light kiss on his cheek. "Let's do it inside in case Andre wakes up."

It was almost an hour before the remaining police car made its way back down the lane. "Wonder what will happen to him?" Andrea cuddled with Andre as he happily gummed a baby biscuit.

Kyle sat down beside them and smiled. He gently stroked Andrea's free arm. "The police told me he's the prime suspect in two murders. The owner of a shooting range was found dead. One of his staff said he was suspicious and asked a few questions. Didn't like the answers, so he asked Sean to leave. A few minutes later, the employee heard shots and ran out. But, Sean had sped off.

"Then, a gas station attendant was killed. The security camera caught it all before Sean shot it out, and because the recording was being done off-site it survived. Sean is going down for life in a locked-down high-security facility. He won't ever get out again." Kyle looked into Andrea's eyes and worked his fingers through her thick locks. He leaned over to give her a long, slow kiss.

"I think I'm going down for life, too," he said, looking over her face.

Andrea smiled and reached up to caress his cheek. "That makes two of us."

Afterword

THE RAND Corporation estimates that there are over 300,000 American military service personnel returning from combat duty in Iraq and Afghanistan who have traumatic brain injuries (TBI). A tragic consequence of inadequately treated TBI is suicide. And, in fact, deaths by suicide now actually outpace combat deaths in the American military, according to published statistics.

TBI is marked by the kinds of symptoms and actions described in this novel. If you know someone who has served and who has these symptoms, please get them to seek treatment. The rate of marriage breakdown, spousal abuse, and violence has reached epidemic proportions. It is particularly difficult for people with TBI who return to combat after their initial injury.

As Andrea said, even civilians have a duty to protect. If you see these symptoms in someone you know or love, please seek help.

TBI can occur after any head injury – a fall, a sports accident, a car accident, a bomb blast. The more "incidents" of brain injury, the worse the cumulative effects appear to be. Someone who played contact sports in high school and college, who then goes on to combat duty could experience multiple TBI that will produce increasingly severe symptoms as more accidents/incidents happen. Remember, Traumatic Brain Injuries tend to be cumulative.

For more information, please visit:

The Brain Injury Recovery Network
National Institute of Neurological Disorders and Stroke
Centers for Disease Control & Prevention
Traumatic Brain Injury.com
SAFE (Stop Abuse for Everyone)

For a first-hand account of the devastating effects of TBI, please visit:

Sheri de Grom to read a 5-part series on TBI from this wife-husband TBI team. Sheri is a passionate advocate for not sending TBI victims back to the front lines.

If You Liked Road to Tomorrow
You'll Enjoy the First Two Books
In the Look to the Future Series...

OTHER BOOKS IN THE SERIES

Winds of Change

After losing her husband and daughter in a plane crash, Boston social worker Jennifer Barrett is rebuilding her life. Finding solace in her work, Jennifer helps young client Mark Powell find work at the seniors' residence where her father lives. After learning Mark hasn't seen his father, an internationally-known broadcast journalist, in over four years, she can't understand how a father could abandon his only son to chase war stories.

When Jennifer meets Ben Powell, she is prepared to dislike him, despite his charm and affable manner. But, when he reveals he's been battling post-traumatic stress disorder, she realizes he didn't want to bring his demons home to Mark, who has suffered from clinical depression. As Jennifer gets to know Ben, she realizes there may be room in her heart for laughter and new love.

Lana Fitzpatrick, a close friend of Jennifer's and a young nurse helping care for Jennifer's father, is also a widow, raising her young son Danny alone. As Lana gets to know her handsome co-worker, Mark Powell, and sees him bonding with Danny, she finds her heart swelling with love.

As new family bonds form, all discover the power of friendship and love to overcome loss so they can face life with renewed hope.

> "Sparkling debut… readers will love being swept along by Winds of Change."
> — JILL ALLEN, CLARION REVIEW

> I loved this book!… it reminded me of Nora Roberts or Jodi Picoult. I could picture everything perfectly as the author described it.
> — CLAIRE MIDDLETON

New Beginnings

Workaholic real estate agent Carol Brock can't seem to find a good man. Her first husband cheated with a law clerk less than half his age. Then she found herself in a string of bad relationships with unscrupulous men, including a con man and art thief, who shredded her professional reputation and strained her relationship with her college-age children. Carol has sworn off men and is determined to reclaim her life and career on her terms. But, when Boston's most eligible bachelor, restoration specialist Devin Elliott, puts in an offer on a charming Victorian, Carol admits she's attracted. Devin's offer unwittingly unleashes a psychopathic rage in an ex-girlfriend that spills into Carol's life. As she and Devin try to stay one step ahead of violence, Carol must decide whether she's ready to risk her heart again.

> *"Mary Metcalfe creates a compelling and compulsively readable story about a woman finding herself again as she writes her second chapter in life. This book has everything: romance, suspense, heart and sizzle!"*
>
> — CARA LOCKWORD,
> *USA TODAY* BESTSELLING AUTHOR

ABOUT THE AUTHOR

Author Mary Metcalfe lives in the foothills of the Laurentians, northeast of Ottawa, Canada with her husband, three cats and a very large dog. Love of writing runs in the family. Their daughter is a published non-fiction author.

Visit *www.lakefrontmuse.ca* to learn more about forthcoming novels and to read excerpts. And drop by her blog: *www.lakefrontmuse.blogspot.com* for weekly interviews with a wide range of authors from around the world.

CPSIA information can be obtained at www.ICGtesting.com
Printed in the USA
BVOW041956281212

309286BV00001B/3/P